Death of My Aunt
C. H. B. Kitchin

"The clues, the ratiocination, and the interplay of feeling among the members of the large family are as effective as the terse, bare prose and the headlong drive of the narrative."

—Jacques Barzun & Wendell Hertig Taylor,
A Catalogue of Crime

Death
of
My Aunt

C. H. B. Kitchin

PERENNIAL LIBRARY
Harper & Row, Publishers
New York, Cambridge, Philadelphia, San Francisco
London, Mexico City, São Paulo, Sydney

Library of Congress Cataloging in Publication Data

Kitchin, C. H. B. (Clifford Henry Benn), 1895-1967.
  Death of my aunt.

  Reprint. Originally published: London : 1929.
  I. Title.
PR6021.I7D4   1984   823′.912   83-48361
ISBN 0-06-080682-6 (pbk.)

84 85 86 87 88 10 9 8 7 6 5 4 3 2 1

TO
MY MOTHER

I

Friday Night: London

UNTIL half-past six, the fifteenth of June was much the same as many other Fridays. Business was slack, and my work did not fill the hours which I had to spend in the office. At six o'clock I took my grimy hat from its peg, and after the innumerable "good-nights" which commercial etiquette seems to demand, walked down Throgmorton Street without enthusiasm on my way to the tube. A few dispirited jobbers still lingered in the "street". The afternoon was wet, and rather cold.

In the train, I looked languidly at the evening paper. The financial pages were dull, and the others were full of heroic achievements, such as Atlantic flights, Channel swims, and rescues from fire—deeds which I knew I could never emulate. I had, indeed, little to look forward to during the weekend. That evening I was to dine in my rooms, after which I was to meet a friend and go with him to the cinema. I had volunteered to go to the office on Saturday morning to help with the books. Beyond this, I had no plans till Sunday afternoon, for which I had invited myself to some friends at Chislehurst. Once or twice I wished I had arranged to stay with my mother and stepfather, who lived at Summer Coombe, a village near Clevedon in Somersetshire. The visit would have given me a change from London, though it could not have been exhilarating. But my married sister, Isobel, was on the verge of having her first baby, and it was clearly my duty to keep away. I have two sisters, both older than myself. The elder one had been married for about a year to a subaltern stationed near Bristol, and had come to my mother's for the great event. My other sister lives aimlessly

5

at home, hoping, I suppose, to marry too. My stepfather, whom my mother had married in 1920, is a clergyman. His living is not worth much. My mother had only three hundred a year in her own right and four hundred under my father's will, and was by no means an economical housewife. Indeed, life at St. Peter's Vicarage, seen from one standpoint, was a series of financial struggles. Isobel's choice of a charming but penniless husband intensified the strain. I myself had one hundred a year under my father's will. The firm of stock-brokers with whom I worked paid me two pounds a week. They admitted that it was only a nominal salary and did not expect much for it. The bulk of my income was supposed to be made out of half-commission, which meant that I had to spend too much time getting aquainted with people with whom I had nothing in common, and being polite to those whom I should have preferred to ignore. My career, however, was of my own choosing, and on the whole I liked it. Money—even other people's—has always interested me.

It was about half-past six when I reached my "bachelor-chambers" in Gloucester Place. I was still thinking about Summer Coombe, and hoping that Isobel would cause no alarm, when, on opening my private front door, I saw a telegram lying on the mat.

"WARREN, 965 Gloucester Place, London, W.
    "Aunt Catherine anxious see you come to-night if possible week-end.
                              "HANNIBAL CARTWRIGHT."

Whenever something had to be done in a hurry, my immediate impulse is to sit down and smoke a cigarette. I did so, and began to consider whether I should obey the summons.

My Aunt Catherine—my only *tante à héritage*, as a friend of mine used to put it—lived at Macebury, a town of about forty thousand inhabitants on the Great Northern line. She was my mother's eldest sister—the most beautiful, at one

6

time, in a family of beauties—and had married a rich man named John Dennis, who died at the end of 1919 and left her with at least half a million. It is true that the business out of which he had made his fortune was not faring well, as I knew from the low price of its shares, but my uncle had died in time for his executors to float it as a public company at the peak of the post-war boom. The proceeds, invested in gilt-edged stocks when they were at their lowest, so far from dwindling, had increased by about twenty per cent. Over this money my aunt had absolute control and absolute power of disposition. By virtue of it, she became queen of the family. It will perhaps save future digressions if I give a list of those who, in 1928, submitted to her rule.

GROUP I.
(a) Mrs. Oldmarsh (my mother), aged (probably) 54, and through her, the Reverend Ambrose Oldmarsh (my stepfather).
(b) Isobel Baldrey (my married sister), 29, and through her, Frank Baldrey, Lieutenant in the South Gloucester Dragoons (my brother-in-law).
(c) Monica Lucy Warren (my unmarried sister), 27.
(d) Myself, 26.

GROUP II.
Hannibal Cartwright, 38, Aunt Catherine's second husband, of whom more anon.

GROUP III.
(a) My uncle, Terence Carvel, 59, formerly barrister on the North-eastern circuit (my mother's only brother). Through him, his wife, Anne Carvel, 47.
(b) Robert Carvel (Bob), 27, son of the above, solicitor, unmarried.
(c) Augusta Teirson, 25, daughter of Terence and Anne Carvel, wife of Sir James Teirson, a penniless baronet twice her age. Permanently resident with her husband in a hovel on the Riviera. No children.

(d) Muriel Carvel, 22, daughter of Terence and Anne Carvel.
(e) Henrietta Carvel, 20, daughter of Terence and Anne Carvel.
All members of this group, except the Teirsons, lived in Macebury.

GROUP IV.
My Aunt, Fanny Carvel, spinster, aged (probably) 56, usually resident at Bude with a school-friend. She had, however, come to Wesley's Hotel, de Vere Gardens, early in June, and was staying there (as far as any of us knew) on Friday, June 15.

GROUP V.
(a) Elizabeth Dennis, spinster, 61?
(b) Harry Dennis, solicitor, 58?, and his plain wife, Mary.
(c) Luke Dennis, solicitor, 55?, unmarried.
(d) Maria Hall, widow, 65?, formerly Maria Dennis, mother of several children, none of whom I had ever met.

The Dennises mentioned in this group are brothers or sisters of John Dennis, Aunt Catherine's first husband. Although John Dennis was a rich man, none of his relations were very well off, and they were sadly disappointed to find, on his death, that they had no reversionary interest in his money. They considered they had a moral claim on Aunt Catherine's estate. Perhaps they had, though, of course, they were not connected with her by blood. Harry and Luke Dennis were moderately prosperous and lived in Macebury. Elizabeth and Maria Hall lived in a tumble-down house eight miles away. Elizabeth had hardly any money of her own, and Maria lived on the irregular doles sent to her by her children. About a dozen of these children were farming in Canada, and I think there were some more in England.

My aunt Catherine, who was, I suppose, just over sixty-three, lived at Otho House. The name used to send us, as children, into hysterical laughter. It was a solid, square house dating from the middle of the last century, and had a garden of six acres, which, on its eastern side, adjoined the principal road running northwards from Macebury. The lodge gates were about a mile and a half from the middle of the town. The inside of the house, except for one or two newly decorated rooms, suggested the Boer War. As a schoolboy I used to spend a large part of my holidays at Otho House, and suffered from Uncle John's Nonconformist conscience. I still remember a wet Sunday in August when my new railway train was confiscated lest I should break the Sabbath. Aunt Catherine never pretended to care for children, and I suppose it was really very kind of her to let me stay with her. I did not enjoy my visits, and as I grew up they became much rarer. After Uncle John's death, Aunt Catherine was such an important person, that her invitations were almost royal commands. They were not very frequent, however, I found, as I grew older, that association with her could be made tolerable if I treated her as a great and experienced personage, deferred to her opinion in everything, and never assumed for myself any knowledge of the world. Nothing was more galling to her than that one should mention an hotel in which she had not stayed, a play which she had not seen, a piece of music which she had not heard. Like many rich people, she acted as if her wealth gave her not only infinite power but infinite wisdom.

Her worst period was about 1922. Just as she was preparing to enjoy Uncle John's money and to move into exalted circles, she developed a painful skin disease in the face, which was badly treated by an incompetent doctor. In the end the trouble was cured, but her looks had almost disappeared, and with them many of her ambitions. It seemed, indeed, as if she had made up her mind to devote herself to her own relations—or rather, that they should devote themselves to her—when, in 1926, she suddenly married a second time.

The family behaved very badly about Uncle Hannibal. I have heard him described as "fortune-hunter", and "member of the lower classes". Aunt Catherine gave out that he was the son of a clergyman, but we translated clergyman by "Nonconformist pastor", and my Uncle Terence declared that Hannibal's real name was Habakkuk. Yet Hannibal suited him better; for there was little of the chapel-goer or even the church-goer, about him. He was a man of under forty, big and well made, with a large square head and face, blue eyes, ginger hair, and moustache. He might have been a physical training instructor. He was clearly attractive to most women, and I always thought the question, "What on earth induced her to marry him?" easily answered. Indeed, I had no doubt that Aunt Catherine married him for what we may call "love".

When she first met him, he was the owner or, more probably, the manager, of the garage in which she kept her car. He played the part, I was told, of the gentleman ruined by the war and forced to turn his hand to trade. My aunt, at the time, had no regular chauffeur, and, as a great privilege, Uncle Hannibal used sometimes to drive her himself. To this honour she responded, particularly on long excursions in the country, by sitting in front with him. There is no doubt that her money attracted him, but it is absurd to say that he married her under false pretences. His charm lay not in his antecedents, but in what he was.

Partly through contrariness and partly because I was glad to see the Carvel vanity affronted, I was my new uncle's only supporter. I think he took me for an ally, and though we had little in common we were friendly from the first. He even entrusted me with five hundred pounds with which to speculate for him, and did not complain when I lost him money. I appreciated it very much, especially as he had so little. Apart from some financial correspondence, my knowledge of him was restricted to three week-ends at Otho House.

Whether I should see the Cartwrights that evening, or Saturday morning, or not at all, I had now to decide. For a while my likes and dislikes fought within me. Why had Aunt Catherine sent for me? Probably just to see if I would come, like M. Jourdain in *Le Bourgeois Gentilhomme*. How much did I want to go to the cinema that evening? How much trouble would it be to undo my arrangements, and telegraph to my mother, if I did go? A telegram to my mother was necessary on Isobel's account. Perhaps I ought not to go so far away? It would be difficult to get from Macebury to Summer Coombe in an emergency. Yet Isobel was a healthy young woman, and even my mother was barely worried. Would Macebury be more boring than an unemployed Saturday afternoon in London? Perhaps. But why had Aunt Catherine sent for me? Curiosity, in the end, made me decide to go.

I rang up King's Cross, and found that I could not catch a train before 8.17. I next wrote a telegram to Uncle Hannibal announcing my arrival, and another telegram to my mother, saying, "Going Otho week-end. Hope all is well." I rang the bell and had these sent off at once. After this, I telephoned to the junior partner in my firm, and as he was out, left a message saying that I was summoned to the bedside of a sick aunt and could not come to the office the next day. This meant that he would have to go himself, but as I knew he was spending the week-end in London it was of small consequence. I had then to get into touch with the friend who was to join me at the cinema, and succeeded after four wrong numbers. It only remained now for me to write a postcard to Chislehurst, pack, and eat a hurried meal. By the time I reached the station, I felt as if I had finished an obstacle race. If I believed in premonitions, I should say that the obstacles were signs against my going.

II

Friday Night: Macebury

THE train arrived punctually, and before I had time to get a porter I found Uncle Hannibal shaking my hand and picking up my heavy bag, which he carried for me to Aunt Catherine's car. Dace, the chauffeur, I noticed, made no attempt to help him when he put the bag on the front seat, and barely returned my "Good-evening". I remembered him with dislike from my last visit—a well-made, wiry little fellow with shrewd eyes.

"It's awfully good of you to come on the spur of the moment," my uncle said, with obsequious friendliness.

"Not at all," I murmured. "It's nice to see you again. How is Aunt Catherine?"

"Oh," he said, "she's really very well. Of course her heart's *not* O.K., but it's nothing to worry about, except I wish she'd lie up a bit more. When you're getting on, you can't take lib——"

He stopped suddenly, as if it occurred to him that Aunt Catherine would have disapproved of his reference to her "getting on". I longed to ask him why she wanted to see me, but thought it wiser to leave him to tell me. Instead, I began to talk about our other relatives with that guilty effusiveness which often attends family reunions.

"I hope Uncle Terence is well?"

"Oh yes. He's been away fishing in Wales for the last week. He's due back in a few days."

"Is Aunt Anne with him?"

"No. She's at home—poor woman."

"Poor woman?"

"Oh, I suppose you haven't heard. Teirson's got into a

silly scrape of some sort at Cannes, and has been threatening to blow his brains out or something. Anne got a wire from Augusta last Saturday, and a letter on Tuesday. Augusta seems to want her mother to go down there. Of course that's out of the question."

"Why?"

"Well, for one thing, I don't think she's fit to travel. As a matter of fact, she went to town to see a specialist to-day. Muriel went with her."

"This is bad news. What is it?"

"I don't quite know. It may be nothing, after all. She gets nervy about herself, I believe."

"I am sorry. I hope it is only her imagination. But oughtn't Uncle Terence to come back, in view of all these troubles?"

"I'm not sure that Terence has been told."

"That's odd, isn't it?"

He did not answer, and I thought it best to change the subject.

"Mother seems quite happy about Isobel," I said.

"Oh, of course, your sister. I meant to ask about her. I'm awfully glad to hear that."

"I rather wondered if I ought to come," I continued, leading to the subject which I wanted him to approach, "in case anything goes wrong, but your wire seemed rather urgent and I thought I'd risk it."

"By Jove, yes. To tell you the honest truth, I'd clean forgotten about Isobel. Just shows how people get out of touch when they live a long way away, doesn't it? I hope you're not upset. Your aunt suddenly wanted to see you, and I thought you mightn't have anything on for the week-end. I'm afraid you must have had a rush. Did you get the wire in good time?"

"When I got home, about half-past six."

"Lord, I thought the Stock Exchange shut at four. That's why I wired to Gloucester Place."

I spent the rest of the drive explaining how, though official

13

dealings stopped at four o'clock, stockbrokers' offices could not close till much later.

"Well, here we are," he said, opening the door and jumping out. Then he turned to Dace.

"Take Mr. Warren's bag upstairs, will you, and unpack it. Is it locked Malcolm?"

"No," I said, amused to notice that Uncle Hannibal called me Mr. Warren to the family servants, while any other relation would have said "Mr. Malcolm". Unobservant with my eyes, I prided myself on seizing psychological *nuances*. Dace gave a grunt which sounded not unlike "Righto", and drove the car round to the garage. Otho House acquired a garage when it acquired Uncle Hannibal. Till that time, Aunt Catherine had been content with my uncle's garage in the town.

My uncle unlocked the front door and we went inside, through a vestibule, where I left my hat, coat and umbrella, into the hall, which, with its nondescript panelling and archaic lighting, reminded me always of one of the less sacred parts of a church.

"How about a spot of whisky before we turn in?"

I agreed gladly. Uncle Hannibal had his merits. John Dennis had been a convinced teetotaler, and had so indoctrinated Aunt Catherine against alcohol that, during her widowhood, she never had any in the house. She had given way to her second husband, and the drinks were openly waiting for us in the drawing-room.

The room which I call the drawing-room should have been, but never was, called the living-room. It occupied the east side of the house, and had windows in the three outside walls. An old but serviceable piano stood on the right of the door, while on the left was a heavy bookcase containing the English Classics in pompous bindings. Neither the bookcase nor the Classics opened easily. A few shelves by the fireplace held lighter literature, dating from 1900.

I sat down on a sofa at right angles to the fireplace though there was no fire, and my uncle sprawled opposite to me in a chair padded in the wrong places, and fitted with arm rests which it was impossible to use. I remember him stretching his big legs and resting his feet inside the marble fender. He looked immensely strong, but a little too stout. It was as if the physical training instructor had been out of work for a week or two and had begun to forget his exercises. I noticed also traces of uneasiness in his manner, and once or twice caught on his face the vacant expression of a distracted mind. I remember wondering lazily, as I saw him sipping his whisky, how he kept himself occupied. The family had been so concerned as to how Aunt Catherine could bring herself to live with him that they never asked how he could bring himself to live with her.

When he spoke a slight thickening in his voice told me that his whisky had been strongly mixed.

"It's a bit hard," he said, "to tell you exactly why I wired for you. Don't exactly know myself. Your Aunt"— (his way of saying "*yer* Aunt" reminded me of my nurse)— "took a craze to see you quite suddenly. It's about her investments, of course."

I repressed a movement of joy. This is what I had been hoping for.

"She read that bit from the paper you sent me," he continued, "and seemed quite struck with it."

I must confess that, in the hope of persuading Aunt Catherine to take a more active interest in the services which I could render her, I had sent Uncle Hannibal a reasonable article on the dangers of letting investments look after themselves for too long. This little piece of touting had been more a matter of form than anything else—an effort to support in print the suggestions which I had let fall verbally from time to time.

"Of course," he went on, "you wonder why she didn't write, or ask me to write, and what's the hurry anyway? But she likes things done quickly, you know. I'm quite in the dark myself. You'd be surprised how little I know about her affairs. Maybe she's going in for a big gamble, though I told her you said it wasn't the time, with New York on the selling tack. But when women are getting on——"

Again the unfortunate phrase stopped him.

"It's exceedingly kind of Aunt Catherine," I said. (My uncle's conversation always made my own stilted.) "In any case, it won't matter whether she wants to do anything or not. I'm very glad to be here. I'll leave her to start the subject."

"Well, there's no need to do that," he replied. "In fact, she thinks you're going to look at her investment book to-night. We expected you a bit earlier, you see, and she got quite worked up. 'Do you think he'll be here by dinner-time?' she kept saying. You wouldn't believe it. In the end I said, 'You go to bed, Catherine. You can't do anything to-night,' but she was so sure you'd want to get to work as soon as you got here that she asked me to hand you this."

He took an envelope from his pocket, gave it to me, and filled his glass. I looked at the envelope with rising excitement. It was sealed with wax, and addressed in pencil to "Malcolm Warren, Esq., *At* Otho House", in my aunt's writing. Inside I could feel something hard, like a key.

"Life's a queer business, Malcolm. I don't know what's in that envelope—key of *yer* Aunt's bureau, most likely. Fact is, I'm not exactly in her confidence; I don't like admitting that, but it's not surprising. After all—no use blinking at matters—I am a bit of an intruder here, and your relations aren't all too eager to see me settling down. At first, I thought we'd all become good pals, but just lately —well, I don't know. Your Uncle Terence never took to me. I don't blame him. He's a cultured man, and had a first-class education. Anne's different, but her children don't care for me either. Bob's hand-in-glove with the Dennis crowd now."

"He's a partner with the two Dennis solicitors, isn't he?"

"Has been, for about a year. Good chap, Bob, but we don't hit it off."

"Nor do I," I said, wishing to repay confidence with confidence.

"Don't you, now? That's queer. You're both the same sort—well-educated——"

"That doesn't count for much. Besides, I don't consider Bob educated, although he went to a good school."

It was unwise of me to talk like this, but Uncle Hannibal's outspokenness had gone to my head, as the whisky had gone to his. It was such a relief, too, to admit that I was not wholly enchanted by the Carvels—(see Group III)—that I exaggerated. In reality I felt for them little but indifference. Uncle Terence had never liked me as a boy. I think he was jealous of my getting a scholarship at Oxford within a few months of his own son's being ploughed for Smalls. Bob was very good at games, and my weakness at them was another sore point with me. Besides, I heard indirectly that he once called me a "pale worm", and this I found hard to forgive. Muriel and Henrietta I detested, partly because they were rude to their mother, whom I admired, and partly because they were always rude to me. I think I can say with fairness that, with the exception of Aunt Anne and Augusta, whose absurd marriage had won my sympathy, they were all conceited. They had some justification. They were all exceedingly good-looking, quick and bright, and had, when they wished, the most attractive manners. In their company my reserved and more introspective nature made me feel something of a kill-joy—always a little too serious. All families have their petty jealousies. At the age of twenty-six, I had outgrown actual ill-will towards my cousins, but I could not feel very tenderly for Uncle Terence, and my mother had not helped to heal the breach by hinting that Bob had had a mistress while articled to some solicitors in London. Unfortunately, the suggestion was too true to be funny.

My uncle put down his empty glass, looked at the decanter and then at me.

"Well," he said, "I expect you want to open *yer* Aunt's

17

letter, and I dare say you're a bit fagged after the week's work and the journey. Like to go up?"

"I think we might. What room am I having?"

"The bachelor's room. A rat died under the floor of the spare room, and they had to take the boards up."

He opened the drawing-room door for me, and turned off the light. When we were half-way upstairs, the telephone bell rang from a recess in the hall. With a muttered apology, my uncle darted past me and attended to the call, while I walked slowly upstairs and groped about for the switch on the landing. Of my uncle's conversation, I only remember the words "going on fine, thanks. . . . Had dinner in her boudoir. . . . Good-night." He joined me just as I had found the switch.

"Ought to have been in bed long ago," he said in a loud whisper.

"Who? Do you mean us?"

"No, that old busybody, Maria Hall. What does she want ringing up at this time of night? She had tea with *yer* Aunt yesterday, and seems to have got scared about her health. This is your room. A bit poky after the spare room, but better than the other little room in front."

The door of my bedroom was a few feet to the west of the head of the stairs. A passage, with a door in either wall, led to a window in the west wall of the house. There was a corresponding passage on the east side of the landing, with one door on the north side and two on the south side, and ending with a fourth door, that of my aunt's bathroom. To the north of this passage was the spare room, in which the rat had died, and to the south were two rooms—my aunt's bedroom, which took up the south-east corner of the house, and another room which I assumed was my uncle's.

"You're in there," I said, pointing to it.

"No," he said, "*yer* Aunt's turned that into a boudoir since you were here. I'm on the other side of you, in the end room. That's the bathroom, opposite my door. We had it put in when *yer* Aunt turned me out, so she has her private bath now. I hope there'll be plenty of hot water in the morning. Has he unpacked properly for you?"

"Oh, that's all right," I said, seeing my things set out in a haphazard fashion.

"You've got h. and c. laid on, you see," my uncle continued. "Well, I hope you'll be comfortable. So long."

He shut the door, and I heard him turn out the light on the landing and go past my door to his own room.

On previous visits to Otho House, I had been given either the spare room or the small room in the north-west corner of the house, which my uncle had referred to as "that other little room in front." The one which I now occupied did not please me. The lights were badly placed, and so also was the furniture, which was too big for the room. There was a large dressing-table in front of the window, the wardrobe almost touching it on one side, and the washstand with its h. and c. on the other. Isolated from these, my bed lay along the wall of the passage, the foot screened from the door by a curtain of blue rep on a frame. The strange grouping was evidently due to the fact that the room had three doors, one leading into the passage, one in the west wall, leading, I supposed, into my Uncle's room, and another in the east wall, leading into the boudoir. Evidently the room was little more than a passage itself.

My first act, after mechanically turning out my pockets and lighting a cigarette, was to read my aunt's letter.

"MY DEAR NEPHEW MALCOLM,

"Your Uncle Hannibal tells me that you expect to arrive about ten o'clock. I shall have gone to bed before that, but send you the key of my bureau in the boudoir—the room next to yours—so that you can have a look at my investment book, if you feel inclined, before you go to sleep. You will find the book lying on the top of the blotter. If you feel tired, leave it till to-morrow. From what your mother tells me, you need have no anxiety over your sister. Sleep well, and come to see me after breakfast.

                    "Your Affectionate AUNT CATHERINE.

"*P.S.*—You will understand that I do not wish my investment book shown to *anyone*, or its contents discussed."

I was by now thoroughly excited. I took the key which I found in a corner of the envelope, and, opening the door between my room and the boudoir as quietly as I could, went to the bureau which I could see was by the window, and unlocked it with agitated fingers. The book was lying on the top of a leather blotter. I lifted it out reverently, shut the bureau, locked it, tiptoed back to my room, and shut the door.

I now began to undress and read the book at the same time. The entries were numerous. The earlier ones, dating from before the death of John Dennis, dealt with small sums, mostly in obscure stocks and shares, which I knew would be difficult to sell. After Uncle John's death, however, the amounts were much larger and the investments of the most reputable kind. I remember sitting on my bed with my shirt half off and calculating, on the back of my aunt's letter, the rough value of her securities. I began, also, to wonder what changes she would let me make, whether she would contemplate an investment in Swedish Match shares, Courtaulds, or Imperial Tobacco, and, if so, how much I should advise her to invest in each. I was, of course, eager to do my best for her, though, after I had put the book in a drawer, turned out the light and got into bed, I could not help calculating my share of the commission on her imaginary orders.

"Five hundred Swedish Match shares at 23. . . . Commission half-a-crown a share. Five hundred half-crowns, sixty-two pounds ten. My share, thirty-one pounds five. Two thousand Courtaulds at four and five-eighths. . . ." The figures whirled in my head, till I decided that it was time to make an effort to go to sleep. Having tried to do so in vain for a quarter of an hour, I realised suddenly that there were far too few clothes on the bed. Except in the hottest weather, I can never get to sleep without a good weight on the top of me, and the single blanket and eiderdown with which I was provided were very insufficient. My silk dressing-gown made no appreciable difference, and I knew that there was nothing for it but to go downstairs and fetch my coat from the vestibule, or a rug if I could find one, to put on the bed. When I visit strange houses, I always try to smuggle my coat upstairs with me to meet this emergency, but in Otho House I had never suffered in this way before.

The door into the passage creaked loudly as I opened it, but I hoped, by creeping very quietly downstairs, not to awaken anyone. There were no rugs to be seen in the vestibule, and I took my coat, in default of better covering. In the hall, I noticed an ash-tray, and took that too, as none was supplied in my room. Then I crept upstairs again, shut my door with great precaution, and got into bed. I suppose it was twenty minutes later that I fell asleep.

Something awakened me in the night, and I remember wondering lazily what the time was. There was no switch by my bed, however, and I was not sufficiently curious to get up in order to turn on the light and look at my watch. A thin shaft of light came from the keyhole of the door into my uncle's room. I listened for a few moments, but, hearing no sound, concluded that he was reading in bed.

III

Saturday: Breakfast

I AWOKE to find my uncle in his pyjamas standing by the doorway between our rooms.

"Is it late?" I murmured, and added, "Good morning." as an after-thought.

"Late?" he said. "Not at all. I didn't mean to wake you if you were still snoozing, but I thought I'd see if you wanted your bath now or after I've had mine."

I was charmed by his solicitude.

"What time is it?"

"Half-past seven."

"Oh, then I think I'll have it later. Is that all right?"

"Quite," he said edging between the wardrobe and the dressing-table, and looking out of the window. "I think it's going to be a fairly decent day. Well, I'll go and have my bath now. I'll tell Dace to call you at a quarter-past eight. Sorry to have disturbed you."

He went back into his room, and I fell asleep again to the sound of running water.

I seemed only to have been asleep for a few seconds, when I was awakened by Dace bustling about the room.

"It's a quarter-past eight," he said, in answer to my greeting. "What suit shall I put out?"

"The oat-coloured one. Plus fours."

"And shirt?"

"Oh, the mauve. Has Mr. Cartwright finished in the bathroom?"

"Mr. Cartwright's dressed and walking in the garden."

"I'd better get up then. You might turn on the bath, will you?"

He nodded and went out. It was not because I was too modest to get out of bed in front of him that I had asked him to turn on the bath. But I suddenly remembered Aunt Catherine's investment book, and thought it wise to lock the drawer in which it was hidden, and take the key with me to the bathroom. I not only disliked Dace for his rudeness, but distrusted him. Before going to the bathroom, therefore, I locked the book up and put the key in my dressing-gown pocket, together with my aunt's letter, which was on the floor beside my bed. I took with me also the bureau key which I found lying on my handkerchief on the dressing-table. Its position struck me as a little odd. Evidently, in my excitement of the night before, I had put the key on the handkerchief instead of the handkerchief over the key.

I had an enjoyable bath, shaved and dressed, and did not forget to transfer the two keys and the letter from my dressing-gown to my day clothes. When I reached the dining-room I found breakfast on the table, and my uncle eating toast and marmalade.

"Did you find what you wanted last night?" he asked.

"You mean the book?"

"Yes."

"Oh yes, quite easily."

"Sleep well?"

"Er—yes."

As he got up to leave the room, I asked him when I should see my aunt. He told me that her tray was taken up about half-past nine, as a rule, and that if I visited her an hour later I should be quite early enough. "I expected she'll want to do a bit of titivating before she sees you," he said.

"I might slip into the town first, then?" I asked. "There's a bus, isn't there, which passes the lodge gates every quarter of an hour?"

"Yes, there is. But if there's anything you want, I'll run you in on my motor-bike. I've got a bike and side-car of my own."

His pride of ownership seemed to me rather pathetic. He was evidently reluctant to order Aunt Catherine's motor.

"I should like that," I said, thinking that it would please him if I admired his toy. "But it will be rather a bore for you, won't it? I wanted to get some papers."

"All right. I'll go round to the garage now and see that she's running well. We use Dace so much indoors that I do odd jobs myself. I'll be round in twenty minutes. That give you time?"

"Rather."

He went out, and I finished my breakfast and looked at the *Morning Post*, which he had put beside my plate. A few minutes later, I heard the motor-bicycle coming round to the front door. It was a shabby little combination, bought by Uncle Hannibal, probably, out of his own savings, without my aunt's assistance. I fetched my hat, and got into the side-car.

"How about some golf this afternoon?" he asked.

"Yes. I haven't brought my clubs, and I'm not like Bob at the game, you know. I expect he's very good, isn't he?"

"I believe so. Haven't played with him myself. I don't play on the town links. I usually go to Fernley, about nine miles out."

Another instance of the cold shoulder, I thought. Poor Uncle Hannibal.

Half-way to the town, we passed Uncle Terence's house.

"I suppose," I said, "I ought to call on the Carvels some time."

"I must stop there on the way back," he said, "as *yer* Aunt asked me to call and see how Anne got on yesterday. Do just as you like. I shall only be a few minutes. But I think Bob will have gone to the office."

"Well, I'll see," I answered. "Perhaps it's rather soon after breakfast to begin paying calls."

24

We reached the shops, and after calling at a stationer's, where I bought the *Financial Times*, the *Investor's Chronicle*, and the *Nation*, I was reminded by a chemist's window, full of patent medicines in brilliant bottles, that I had forgotten to bring a nail-brush with me. The one which I had left in London was almost worn out, and I decided to buy a new one. My uncle did no shopping for himself, but waited about at my convenience. It was ten minutes past ten when we stopped at Yew House, where the Carvels lived. Rather than risk being caught by Muriel and Hetty while waiting for my uncle, I started to walk on to Otho House, expecting him to overtake me. He did not do so, and I arrived at Otho House before half-past ten. There, after preparing one or two little speeches while taking a turn in the garden, I went up to my room, put the nail-brush, still in its wrappings, on the dressing-table, and knocked at my aunt's door.

IV

My Aunt

(Saturday, 10.40 A.M.)

A GRACIOUS voice bade me come in, and I found my aunt propped up by pillows in her large bed. She was wearing a gay little boudoir cap of cream-coloured lace, with a tassel hanging roguishly by the left ear, and a silk bedroom jacket of the same colour, ornamented with lace on sleeves and collar. Round her neck, which was much exposed, was a string of large pearls. I have never seen her look so charming since I was a child. Her skin was carefully powdered and rouged. A charitable eye might have taken her for under forty.

She held out her hand, and when I approached to shake it gave me a kiss, which I returned. After I had said a few words of greeting and admiration, which she enjoyed, she told me that I was looking pale, and should try to get fatter.

"But I suppose slim figures appeal to people nowadays," she said.

"By no means always," I answered, giving her a gallant smile.

We continued in this strain for a short time. Her mood was one of which I had no experience in her. I could remember her as a beautiful and stately creature, ready to keep children at a distance, and also, at the time of her husband's death, a tragic sufferer, clutching at her heart and speaking of her "great sorrow". Later, during her illness, she had been morose and sometimes savagely bitter, and later still she became a lady bountiful, queen of her family and supreme arbiter of conduct. Now she had changed once more, and seemed in her old age to have slipped back into

26

girlhood. There was about her something arch and deliberately feminine, rare in these days, perhaps, but common, I
suppose, in 1890. Even her bedroom had been altered since
I had seen it. The walls had been stripped of paper and
painted a pale yellowish pink. The floor was parquet, and
the old Brussels carpet had made way for three Persian rugs.
The glass top of the walnut dressing-table was covered with
scents and trinkets. By the bed stood a beautiful sofa-table,
on which were a bowl of roses, some notepaper in a lac-
quered stand, a large blotter made of old red morocco, and
an elaborate china ink-pot fitted with coloured quill-pens.
The head of the bed was covered with a deep scarlet Italian
brocade. I was amazed at the contrast between the room and
the rest of the house, with its deliberate neglect of elegance
and comfort, its acquiescence in dead fashion and dead ways
of thought.

Yet I was not deceived into believing that my aunt was
altogether changed. She had never changed in two things, her
desire for the immediate fulfilment of her wishes, and her
wish to rule—and each of her past phases, however self-
contradictory they seemed, were but the outward signs of a
fixed nature. I saw also that, though at the moment she was
pleased to purr, she still had claws with which she could
scratch.

I sat down in an armchair near the bed, and we talked
about my mother, and my sister, and my life in London. Of
this I was careful to say nothing which could make her
envious—not, indeed, that on this score there was much to
say—and replied to some coquettish innuendoes with an
innocence as coquettish. She did not mention Uncle Hannibal, nor did I, except to say that he had given me bad news
of my aunt Anne Carvel. At that she frowned, half in pain
and half in displeasure, and said, "Yes, yes. Poor woman. It's
very sad, too sad. . . . People always come to me with their
troubles. I could wish sometimes for livelier visitors. I have
my troubles too, but deal with them myself. There are times,
Malcolm, when I should like to forget my responsibilities

27

and run away to some new place and make new friends. Well, that I suppose can never be. . . ."

I sighed in sympathy.

"I'm afraid," she went on, "I was born impatient. When I want things done, I want them done at once. Perhaps I am making up for lost time. I am full of new plans and ideas. You got my letter?"

"Yes. I have it here."

"Did you find the book?"

"Yes. I read it with great interest. I was so excited I could hardly sleep."

Her expression changed momentarily, and a grim, almost cruel look, with which I was not unfamiliar, came over her face.

"I shall be only too glad," she said, "if I can leave my investments as they are."

I felt her eyes searching mine for a trace of disappointment.

"Of course you can," I replied as carelessly as I could. "All your important holdings are absolutely secure, and in your position, it is hardly worth while troubling about the few pounds you have in local preference shares."

"Hardly worth your while either?"

"Barely. As for the other things, it depends what you want to do. If you want to use your money to make more, you will have to choose a different type of investment. But from what I have seen of your book, I shouldn't think you have any use for a larger income."

She was clearly surprised at my plain speech, and, I thought, uncertain whether or not to be angry.

"There are many calls on my income of which you know nothing," she said.

"In that case, security of income must come first."

"Ye—es, of course. In part. But perhaps you realise that I have very large sums at my disposal?"

"I do."

"Mind, Malcolm, I have taken you completely into my

confidence over my affairs. You are never to disclose them to anyone. If you do, I shall not forget it or forgive you. You understand?"

"Quite. I have seen your investment book in my professional capacity."

The phrase sounds intolerably pompous, but it was not unsuitable when said.

"You are my only relative to know what you do. Of course the Dennises, the solicitors, attended to your Uncle John's will, and know what he left—in *their* professional capacity. I have no reason to suppose that they have ever——"

"Of course they haven't."

"Well then—now tell me, Malcolm, what would you do, what prospects should I have, if I entrusted you with a hundred thousand pounds to use for me?"

This time I was really startled. Despite my elation of the previous night, I had anticipated the somewhat grudging offer of a few hundred pounds, which with the exercise of infinite caution, I was to turn into ten thousand. With a hundred thousand to manipulate. I saw myself becoming at last someone of importance. In a flash I pictured my improved status in the office, perhaps a partnership. But my aunt was watching me narrowly.

"I must have a little time," I said, "to think of my answer. And I must know first exactly what you would allow me to do with the money. For example, if you insisted that——"

There was a knock at the door, and Buxey, my aunt's personal maid, came in with a jug of hot drinking water and a tumbler, which she put down on the sofa-table. I think my aunt and I were both glad to have the tension relaxed for a moment; for when Buxey had gone out, Aunt Catherine said, "That reminds me. I must send off a note to Canon Hurdler before twelve. I shan't take long."

I rose from my chair, and was walking idly round the room, when my aunt opened the morocco blotter and gave a cry of annoyance.

"That wretched girl," she said. "I told her yesterday to put some blotting-paper here as well as in the drawing-room. I wonder if you'd mind fetching me some. You'll find plenty in the blotter in my bureau. Did you put the book back in the bureau after reading it last night?"

"No, I kept it locked up in a drawer in my dressing-table," I answered. "I've got the key and the bureau key here."

"Well you might fetch the book at the same time. I generally keep it in the bottom drawer of the bureau, but put it on the top so that you should find it easily. We may want to look at it, mayn't we? That side door's unlocked."

She pointed to a door in the west wall of her room, half-hidden by an old French screen. I opened it, and went straight through the boudoir into my bedroom beyond. There I took out the precious book, and left the key of the drawer in the key-hole. Then I returned to the boudoir, and unlocked the bureau. Lying on the top of the blotter was a flat bottle of pink glass not unlike a large scent-bottle, wrapped round with a pamphlet. I had not noticed it when I had taken the book, the night before. I put the bottle on the top of the bureau, and took two sheets of blotting-paper from the blotter. I then locked the bureau, and was about to return to my aunt's bedroom, when I remembered the bottle, which I had left out. The wide neck bore an ornate label with the words, "Le Secret de Venus", in gold letters. The title amused and puzzled me, and accorded so well with my aunt's mood earlier in the morning that I thought it safe to tease her with my discovery.

"I've found the blotting-paper," I said when I got back into her room, "and something else. Look!"

She took the blotting-paper, and gave a nervous little laugh as I brandished the bottle.

"Oh, you naughty boy. Have you been rummaging among my treasures? Give it to me at once."

"What is it?"

"It's a tonic—a very special tonic. I meant to take a dose this morning."

She snatched the bottle from me, took out the stopper, poured some hot water into the tumbler, and emptied some white crystals, not unlike Epsom salts, into it.

"There," she said, pointing to the pamphlet which I retained in my hand. "You can read what that says while I finish my letter. I'm not sure, though, that it's very suitable for a young man. Perhaps we'd better tear it up."

"Oh," I said, "you must let me read it first."

She pursed her lips with mock solemnity. "I'm afraid in parts it's almost improper. But perhaps you won't understand that."

She took up her pen again, and I sat down in the armchair. The pamphlet, like those accompanying many patent medicines, was in several languages. More than that, the account in each language was divided into two parts. The first part had an air of great seriousness, and referred to the universal interest taken in the product by the medical profession. There was great talk of vitamins, lipoids, and other substances of which I had never heard, followed by testimonials from foreign nerve-specialists and gynæcologists. The second part of the prospectus was very different, and evidently aimed at appealing to the lay reader. After touching on the strain of modern existence, and the crucial age in the life of "lovely woman, who, with her spirit still young and ardent, finds to her dismay that the years have begun to dim the natural fires of her body," it spoke of a great secret possessed by Aspasia, Catherine Parr, Lady Hamilton (spelt "lady Amilton"), and the renowned Dubarry, all of whom had "played a part in the destinies of great nations and great men." This secret, in more perfect form, was contained in the "magic crystals." "After four doses," I read, "you will feel a new zest for life, and love, and laughter; a new urge. The withered charms will blossom again, the glow of youth return."

I looked up and saw my aunt raise the tumbler to her lips and take a sip.

"Oh, what a horrible taste," she said. "I didn't think

31

it was so bitter—*mais toujours, toujours, il faut souffrir pour être belle!*"

She gave me a sweet little smile, and lay back on the pillow, shutting her eyes, in order, I supposed, that she might enjoy the "new urge" without being distracted from it by my conversation. As for me, I turned to the second half of the French version, hoping that it would be freer than the English translation. It contained some pretty phrases, and when I had finished it I went on idly to the languages which I knew less well—German and Italian. I was just starting on the latter, when I was appalled to hear a loud moan from my aunt, who sat up with a convulsive movement and was violently sick.

To recall what next happened I have to use my reason. My actual memory of those nightmarish moments is still confused. My first act, I think, must have been to run over to the bell by the fireplace. The spasms continued and became more horrible. I believe I took my aunt's hand for a moment, and then ran to the bell again. At length Buxey came in, and stood aghast by the door. "Mrs. Cartwright has been suddenly taken ill," I said. "What can we do?" and as the terrified woman went to the bed I rushed downstairs and found Dace in the pantry.

"Has Mr. Cartwright come in?" I asked.

"Not yet. Leastways I haven't heard his machine."

Even at that moment, I was annoyed at his refusal to say "Sir".

"Then go and telephone at once for Mrs. Cartwright's doctor," I said. "Tell him that Mrs. Cartwright is having a most alarming attack. Don't leave the telephone till you get into touch with him, or some other doctor. When you've got him, ring up Mr. Carvel's house and find out if Mr. Cartwright is still there. But get a doctor first."

When I saw that he was going to do as I told him, I ran upstairs again, and found Buxey loosening my aunt's clothes and patting her hand. The nausea had ceased, and my aunt was lying down, gasping and trembling. The bed was in a horrible state, and the bowl of roses and tumbler had been knocked off the sofa-table. I approached in an agony of incompetence.

"The doctor will soon be here," I said, and tried to smile reassuringly. For three or four minutes nothing happened, and then my aunt seemed to shudder with her whole body and suddenly lay quite still.

"She's fainted," I said, "or——"

Buxey, who had by now recovered her self-possession, looked at me gravely, and said, "I'm afraid it's worse than that, sir." Then, while I turned away instinctively, she felt my aunt's heart. "I'm afraid the poor lady's gone, sir."

I went to the armchair and sat down weakly.

"Can't we do anything?" I asked.

She shook her head, and told me that her little experience of nursing left her no doubt but that my aunt was dead.

I suddenly felt that I should be sick if I stayed in the room any longer.

"Perhaps," I said timidly, "you wouldn't mind staying here while I see if Dace has got through to the doctor?"

She pulled a chair to the bedside, and sat down.

I met Dace on the stairs.

"I was coming to say I've got into touch with Dr. Bradford. He was due at Mrs. Mitchell's house—that's right the other side of the town—and I caught him there. He should be here in twenty minutes. There's a good deal of traffic in the town, and he'll have to go slow. How is Mrs. Cartwright?"

"Your mistress is dead," I said, and brushing past him went down into the drawing-room. There I sat down, and felt in my pocket for my cigarette case. In taking it out, I found with it the pamphlet on the Secret of Venus. I threw the latter disgustedly into the fender, and lit a cigarette. Then —to my surprise, I burst into tears. It was evidently a physical reaction, for beyond my natural horror at the terrible scene I had just been through, I had no real sorrow for the loss of my aunt, and had even then, though it is painful to admit it, begun to wonder what changes her death would bring about. However, my tears flowed unceasingly, and after a time almost amused me. It was as if I were watching a burst pipe that no one could stop up.

I looked at my watch. It was nearly half-past eleven. The doctor would be arriving in about a quarter of an hour, and I decided to wait about for him in the drive. I forgot to ask Dace if he had telephoned to my uncle at the Carvels.

The drive at Otho House winds to the main road in pretentious curves. I had just walked a quarter of the distance to the gates, when I saw my Uncle Hannibal on his motor-bicycle. He stopped on seeing me, and, noticing my distressed appearance, ran up to me and said, "What on earth's the matter, old chap? You look as if you've seen a ghost."

"Aunt Catherine . . ." I answered. "I'm afraid I have bad news. Aunt Catherine is dead."

To my great exasperation, I burst into a new fit of sobbing. He put his arm round, me and we walked across the grass to the house without speaking.

V

The Doctor

(Saturday, 11.30 A.M.)

WHEN we reached the house, my uncle rushed upstairs, where, I suppose, he saw Buxey for a moment, and came down again. Before asking me any questions, he got me a whisky and soda, and one for himself. He was pale, but calm, though I was too occupied with my own hysteria to pay much attention to the way he received my news. Besides, the drink went to my head, and I had a feeling of detachment and irresponsibility. Beyond the fact of my aunt's sudden seizure, and my instructions to Dace, I had little to tell him.

"Did Dace get through to you at the Carvels?" I asked.

"He couldn't have. I only stayed there about ten minutes, and went off for a little spin in the country. When exactly did this convulsion begin? What were you both doing at the time?"

I told him about the Secret of Venus, and said that I had been reading the pamphlet while my aunt digested the drink. I pointed to the fender where the pamphlet was lying. Then, for the first time, it occurred to me that there might have been a connection between the drink and my aunt's death.

"I suppose," I said, "it must have been a heart attack."

"I suppose so," he answered. "But that's the doctor's business."

At that moment we heard the doctor's car. My uncle went to the front door, while I remained in the drawing-room. Soon afterwards I heard them going upstairs. I took a book at random—I have no idea what it was—from the shelf containing light literature, and turned over the leaves. "After all," I thought, "it's over now. The main thing is to have as little fuss as possible."

35

A few minutes later Buxey came in and told me that the doctor wished to see me. He was in the boudoir. I went up, and my uncle introduced me to him. He was a cross-looking little man, with big ears and a small grey moustache. If I had been his patient, I should have feared that he was not telling me the whole truth about myself.

"I'm sorry to trouble you," he said, "but I must ask you a few questions."

"Do you want me to stay?" my uncle asked.

"As you like."

My uncle went out, and the doctor signed to me to sit down.

"When did you first see your aunt this morning?" he asked.

"A little after half past ten."

"Did you see her last night?"

"No. I arrived late."

"How was she when you first saw her? Did she seem herself? In good spirits?"

"In remarkably good spirits."

"What was the nature of your conversation with her? Was it exciting, or distressing?"

"Not at all distressing. A little exciting, perhaps, though I think I was the one to be excited. It was about finance, mostly."

"H'm. You are in business?"

"I am in a stockbroker's office."

"There was nothing you said which could have agitated Mrs. Cartwright?"

"Nothing," I answered, and I described the subsequent events with greater fullness than I had to my uncle. He listened to me without comment, and said "Thank you" when I had finished.

"I suppose," I said, "it was a heart attack?"

"Mrs. Cartwright certainly died of heart-failure."

"Could it have been brought on by the drink, do you think?"

"At present I am not prepared to say."

At that he gave me a severe look and went into my aunt's bedroom. I was a little annoyed at his mystery-making. "No doubt," I thought on my way downstairs, "he is upset because she didn't die according to the rules. Probably he never realised how seriously ill she was."

I said something of the sort to my uncle, who was sitting by the drawing-room writing-table. He made no comment, and I began to wonder how far he was affected merely by shock, and how far by real grief. Of myself I had now no doubt. My own nervous agitation in no way resembled the hopeless misery which I had once felt on the death of a friend to whom I was devoted. My uncle seemed to be concerned as to whom he ought to tell of what had happened, and how. Here I felt I could be of use to him, and offered to draft some telegrams.

"Terence must be told," he said, "and, I suppose, your mother and Fanny."

"Do you know Terence's address?"

"No."

"Then I'd better tell Bob, and let him send word to his father."

"Thanks awfully, old man."

"He'll be at the office still, will he? It's not twelve yet."

"I should think so."

I went to the telephone, rang up the firm of Dennis and Carvel and asked for Mr. Robert Carvel. A voice, which I thought belonged to one of the brothers Dennis—I had not seen either of them for years—told me that Mr. Robert Carvel had left a few minutes earlier for the station, and that he was spending the week-end in Hertfordshire. I was then asked who I was, but pretended not to hear, and rang off. I had no wish just then to begin a conversation with my marriage-connections, and did not care even to give them my news, without instructions from my uncle.

There was nothing for it but to telephone to my Aunt Anne, ill though she might be; for I judged Muriel and

Henrietta too irresponsible. It was Aunt Anne herself who answered me.

"Good morning, Malcolm," she said. "Uncle Hannibal told me you had come."

I delivered my message in awkward phrases. She gave a little gasp, and said, "Oh, I am sorry—I am so very sorry. Is there anything I can do?"

"Only to telegraph to Uncle Terence. He ought to know as soon as possible."

"I will, at once. But if he's out for the day, fishing. . . . Still we shall have done what we can. How was it, Malcolm, that it happened?"

"It was heart-failure."

"Was the doctor there?"

"No. He came too late to do anything. He's in the house now."

"I'll come and see you, if I can, this afternoon. After tea. Unless—perhaps you'd come here?"

"I will, if I can."

"I am so sorry—and for you. What a terrible shock it must have been."

There was a pause, and she said good-bye and rang off.

I went into the drawing-room again and wrote out telegrams to my mother and Aunt Fanny. While I was doing so, I heard the doctor come downstairs and go to the telephone. When he had finished, my uncle joined him in the hall, and I heard their voices through the open door.

"I've telephoned for a nurse," the doctor said, "and she ought to be here in half an hour."

"Thank you. Meanwhile I'd better get the room put to rights?"

"No. I wish nothing to be touched or rearranged in any way. In fact, I have taken the liberty of locking the doors."

"How about the nurse getting in, then?"

"I shall call at the infirmary and give her the key. I shall be coming back myself as soon as I can. I have to make a further examination, and shall require some—er—extra apparatus."

"Oh, then perhaps you'll have lunch with us?"

"Thank you, but I think I shall be able to get home by two. In any case, I don't want to trouble you."

The front door shut, and I heard the sound of the doctor's motor. When my uncle came into the drawing-room again he looked both embarrassed and puzzled.

VI

The Police

(Saturday, luncheon)

ALREADY the morning had seemed inordinately long, and the remaining hour before luncheon passed even more slowly. My uncle apparently did not need me, and I went out into the garden, where I strolled aimlessly. It is extraordinary how quickly one's moods—even moods of great intensity—can change. I now found myself slightly resentful of what had happened, impatient of the strain which I saw was going to be imposed upon me, and eager for a resumption of normal life, in which one could be openly amused. I had never before been in a house in which a death occurred, and did not realise the demands which it was bound to make upon social intercourse. I even felt it a piece of humbug that my uncle and I should be deprived of our golf that afternoon.

I saw the nurse arriving in a motor while I was sitting under some trees near the drive. As far as I could gather from my glimpse of her, she was a purposeful woman of thirty-five—the type, I reflected unjustly, to clamour for steak and onions three times a night in a house of sickness. The motor stopped at the front door, where she got out. I presume she was shown upstairs by my uncle; for I did not see her when I went back to the house.

It was chilly where I was sitting, and I walked briskly to the kitchen garden, which lay on the west side of the house, beyond the garage. I picked and ate a fair number of peas. They were small and not quite ripe. I remember once asking myself to whom they, and the rest of Otho House, now belonged. While I was still devouring the substance of the unknown heir, I heard another motor in the drive, which I concluded must be the doctor's, though the engine sounded very powerful for his little two-seater. I was in no hurry to meet him again, and stayed where I was till he should have gone upstairs. When I passed the front door on my way back to the French window, I saw that, if it was the doctor who had come, he must have changed his car, for this was a big and shabby Daimler, with room for seven or eight persons.

My uncle was still in the drawing-room, sitting in an armchair and fingering his moustache nervously; when I came in, he stood up and made a noise in his throat.

"The doctor's come back," he said, "and brought the police."

"The police?" I repeated stupidly.

"The police-surgeon, Dr. Mathews, Inspector Glaize, and a constable."

"But—why?"

"How the hell should I know? Bradford came in and said something about not being at all satisfied, and feeling unable to dispense with an inquest. He introduced me to his friends, and they all went upstairs together. They'll be wanting to see us both in a few minutes. In fact they asked me to find you in the garden."

"Really," I said, "this is too——" and stopped, while my mind, like a flower suddenly subjected to some intense electrical ray, broke into strange bloom. New thoughts and conjectures shot up within me, incoherent and alarming.

At that moment Dr. Bradford came in without knocking.

"I am exceedingly sorry to tell you," he said, "that neither Dr. Mathews nor I have any doubt but that Mrs. Cartwright met her death through an unnatural cause. Inspector Glaize would like to see Mr. Warren at once—in the boudoir."

Without speaking or looking at the two men, I went upstairs.

The Inspector introduced himsef to me at once. I found him even less prepossessing than Dr. Bradford. He was a fat man, with a large damp face, watery blue eyes, and a red nose. His hair was thin and grey. A policeman in uniform stood by him, handsomely sunburnt.

"Will you please sit down, Mr. Warren?"

He pointed to a chair facing the window. The old trick, I thought.

"This is a shocking business, sir," he began, when I had taken up my position. "No doubt Dr. Bradford has informed you that he felt bound to order a post-mortem of the deceased, owing to certain suspicions which he formed at an early stage. These suspicions, I may say, are fully shared by Dr. Mathews, our police-surgeon. There is no harm in my telling you—in fact, it is my duty to tell you—that Mrs. Cartwright met her death through poison. The poison has still to be tested, but the medical gentlemen are agreed in suspecting it of being oxalic acid, and of having been concealed in a preparation known as 'Le Secret de Venus'."

He pronounced "secret" in the English way.

"This preparation," he went on, "is a quack mixture, quite innocent in itself, and could not by any possibility produce harmful consequences. You see"—and here his manner became less formal and more confidential, "I'm putting all my cards on the table, sir, because I want your help. There is no doubt that the poor lady met her death by foul means, and I am sure you are as eager as we are to get at the truth. I understand that you were the only person present in the room when she took the mixture and when the poison began to show its effects. I shall of course question everyone in the house, but I should first like to have an account, in your own words, of all that happened after you went into Mrs. Cartwright's room this morning."

I told my story for the third time, still more fully than before.

"The investment book, now? Would that be the leather-bound book we found on the settee at the foot of the bed?"

"Yes. I must have put it there when my aunt took the mixture."

For a moment I felt quite guilty of my carelessness. But

what, after all, did it matter if the nurse, Dr. Bradford, and the police doctor had all read it?

"Go on, please."

I continued my account to the time when I went downstairs, leaving Buxey in the room.

"What do you say were Mrs. Cartwright's last words?"

"Her last words, unless she uttered some during the attack, which I did not catch, were: '*Toujours, toujours, il faut souffrir être belle*'."

"H'm. French, I suppose. And what did you take those words to mean?"

"I took them to mean, 'Always, always, it is necessary to suffer in order to be beautiful'."

"What did you understand by the reference to suffering?"

"I thought it was a reference to the bitter taste of the drink."

"You are sure that Mrs. Cartwright didn't mean that she was suffering because she *was* beautiful?"

"Quite sure."

"Wasn't it a rather peculiar thing to say?"

His way of snapping the question at me irritated me. How can these people hope to succeed, I thought, if they will judge everything from the "plain man's" standpoint?

"I thought the remark quite in keeping with my aunt's mood."

"You say that when you mentioned Mrs. Carvel, your aunt referred to troubles of her own. Have you any idea what they were?"

"None."

"Nothing to do with money?"

"Certainly not. My aunt was a very wealthy woman."

"But she said she had many calls upon her?"

"Yes."

"What did you take that to mean, Mr. Warren?"

"I thought she was alluding to her poor relations."

"Did Mrs. Cartwright make you an allowance?"

"No."

"But you had presents from her—money presents?"

"Yes."

"Fairly regularly?"

"At Christmas and on my birthday."

"Excuse me if I ask for what amount?"

"Usually for £50."

"Will you also excuse my asking if £50 means a good deal to you, sir?"

"It does."

"Do you know any other members of the family to whom Mrs. Cartwright gave allowances—or handsome presents?"

"My mother, and my sisters, on a smaller scale. And I think my unmarried aunt Fanny Carvel. I dare say others, too."

"Supposing these troubles were not money troubles, what could they be?"

"I have no idea."

"You hadn't the curiosity to ask?"

"No."

"Did it surprise you that Mrs. Cartwright mentioned having troubles?"

"Not very much."

"Why not?"

I was again irritated.

"Most women, especially elderly women, have their grievances," I said, "and rather enjoy having them."

"I see. You are a student of human nature. How old are you?"

"Twenty-six."

"I want you now to tell me what opinion you formed of the relations between your aunt and Mr. Cartwright."

"I'm not sure that I formed any opinion."

"Come, come, Mr. Warren. You want to help us, don't you? Did they get on well together?"

"I have only seen them together a very few times."

"How often?"

"When I spent a week-end here in November of last

44

year, another week-end in the early spring of that year, and another in October 1926."

"How did they get on in October 1926?"

"Very well."

"And in the spring of 1927?"

"Very well."

"And last November?"

"Very well."

"Quite as well as during the two earlier week-ends?"

"If you press me, I suppose I must say 'Not quite'. But I don't wish to imply that there was any kind of breach or ill-feeling."

"What made you think that they were not getting on quite so well?"

"Only that they weren't so much in one another's company—and perhaps some very trivial incidents which may have combined to give me an impression, though I can't remember any of them."

"On the whole, you would say that the marriage was very successful?"

"Yes, considering the difference of age and tastes, I should say it was as successful as most marriages."

"You take a cynical view of marriage, perhaps?"

"I don't imagine husbands and wives live in a state of perpetual bliss."

"You are unmarried?"

"Yes."

There was a pause, during which the Inspector looked at some notes. I lit a cigarette, without asking permission to smoke. Glaize had by now succeeded in making me antagonistic to him. I was particularly annoyed by the way in which he seemed to set himself up as a standard of conduct and to assume that any act which surprised him must also surprise others. He set no store, as I was to realise more fully later, by the waywardness of human nature, made no allowances for the innumerable irrational acts habitually performed by rational people, had no conception of the mass

45

of habits and inhibitions which continually regulate, unawares, the behaviour of the most normal. He would, I was sure, be suspicious of any plea of absent-mindedness, momentary indecision, sudden revulsion. In short, I felt he might learn much from me.

"I now wish to ask you," he said, "a few questions about the bottle containing this preparation. When did you first see it?"

"When I went to the bureau to get the blotting-paper."

"It was lying, you said, on its side, on the top of the blotter in the bureau. Had you previously looked into the bureau?"

"Yes, last night." I then told him about my aunt's letter, and my finding of the investment book.

"The book was on the blotter?"

"Yes."

"Beside the bottle, or on the bottle?"

"I saw no bottle last night."

"Are you quite sure? This may be important. I want you to think carefully."

"I don't remember seeing it or feeling it."

"Feeling it?"

"I didn't turn on the light in this room. I wasn't quite sure where the switch was."

"You groped about in the dark?"

"Quite a lot of light came through that door, which I left open. It didn't fall directly on to the bureau, but I was able to see the outline of the book."

"Wouldn't it have been simpler to strike a match and look for the switch?"

"Much simpler, probably. But I didn't do it."

"How did you know you'd get the right book?"

"It was the only book there. When I took it to the light, of course, I knew at once."

"Then the bottle might have been there without your seeing it?"

"Perhaps—though I don't think so. At any rate, not on the top of the blotter."

"You are not very observant?"

"I don't try to record all the stray impressions received by my eyes and ears. I should regard that as a waste of time, bad for the imagination and stultifying to the intelli——"

"Possibly. But you would think you would have remembered the bottle if it had been where you found it this morning?"

"Yes. I do."

"When you looked at the bottle, was it full?"

"I don't know. There is a band of coloured paper round the neck."

"But when it was lying on its side, you might have been able to tell."

"I didn't notice. I have somehow the impression that it was full, or very nearly."

"Was there anything over the stopper, to keep it on?"

"I don't think so."

"Did you take out the stopper?"

"No, my aunt did."

"Had she any difficulty in doing so?"

"None that I saw."

"Very well. Now I want you to tell me this. Have there been any events since your arrival which you regard as unusual or suspicious, or which you now so regard?"

"The position of the bottle on the blotter, perhaps."

"Yes, yes. We have gone through that. Anything else?"

"No. Nothing."

"You are quite sure?"

"Yes."

There was another pause. Then he said, suddenly, "Thank you, Mr. Warren. That will be all for the present, though, I may, of course, have to ask you some further questions later. Meanwhile, I'm afraid I must ask you not to leave the house or grounds without getting permission from Constable Hare, who will be about or near the premises."

"Very well. Do you think I shall be able to leave here on Sunday night, or Monday morning?"

"I'm afraid I can say nothing definite. By the way, as a pure matter of form, of course, will you oblige me by letting me take your finger-prints?"

"Certainly."

He took two sheets of paper from an attaché-case, and made me press the fingers of both hands on them, in various positions.

"Thank you, sir. Hare, will you go down and ask Mr. Cartwright to come up?"

I said good-morning and left the room, followed closely by the policeman. In the hall we met Dace, who told me that my uncle was having lunch in the dining-room.

"What a time they've kept you," my uncle said, when I opened the door. "You must excuse me beginning."

Before I could reply, the policeman pushed past me and said, "Mr. Cartwright, the Inspector would like to see you immediately, sir, if you please."

My uncle gave me a look, and went out of the room, the policeman following.

As I sat down at the table, I had the feeling that Inspector Glaize considered me a hostile witness.

VII

My Eavesdropping

(*Saturday, after luncheon*)

LUNCHEON was cold, and carelessly set out. I began hungrily, but after a few mouthfuls had to make an effort to eat. My thoughts were painfully adjusting themselves to a new set of circumstances. No longer had I any prospect of a calm, if tedious, week-end. It was not even sufficient that I should school myself to good behaviour in the presence of death. I had been plunged into a drama such as I had no experience of save in print. I was confronted with strange forces, to match which I had to evoke qualities in myself either dormant or non-existent. The truth of the situation was conveyed to me in fragments, a jig-saw puzzle presented in disorder. And I had no certainty that many pieces were not still missing.

I soon lost patience with my poor appetite. My uncle was being questioned upstairs, and likely to remain there for some time. I thought of going into the garden with a book, but a shower threatened. Instead, I decided to lie down in my room. The idea that I might overhear what was being said in the boudoir was not consciously present to me, but I must have had some sense of performing a guilty action, for I crept up the stairs very quietly and opened and shut my bedroom door with precaution. As I lay down, I could distinctly hear the sound of voices. The head of my bed only just missed trenching on the space occupied by the door into the boudoir, and I found that by rearranging my posture I could place my head near enough to the keyhole to gather most of what was being said in the next room. If disturbed, I had a fair excuse for being where I was.

The first words I caught were spoken by Glaize.

"Was this bureau generally kept locked?"

To this my uncle's voice replied, "I think so."

"How do you mean, you think so?"

"It was my wife's private bureau, and I did not tamper with it."

"Do you mean to say you have never opened it?"

"I wouldn't say that."

"When was the last time you opened it?"

"I can't remember."

"Was it to-day, or yesterday?"

"No."

"During the past week?"

"No."

"Or month?"

"I think not."

"Where did your wife keep the key?"

"In her bag, perhaps. I really don't know."

"Where did she take it from when she put it in the envelope addressed to your nephew?"

"I don't know. I wasn't there. I wasn't even sure that it was the key of the bureau."

"How did you know it was a key?"

"It felt like one. Besides, she told me she had arranged for my nephew to get at the book."

"Weren't you surprised that your wife didn't give you the book straight out, and ask you to give it him?"

"Not altogether."

"Why not?"

"Well, my wife was always rather—close, I might call it—about money matters. She didn't want people to know how much she had."

"Not even her husband?"

"No."

"When did you first see the bottle containing the pre-paration?"

"When I went to my wife's bedroom with the doctor. At least, that's when I might have seen it first."

"What do you mean?"

"I might have seen it when I rushed upstairs for a minute after coming in. I don't remember seeing it very clearly. I was naturally very much taken aback by——"

"Quite so. Can you describe the bottle?"

"It was of pink glass, rather like a fancy scent-bottle about five inches high——"

"How can you describe it so well if you don't remember seeing it?"

"I suppose I must have seen it—or my nephew told me what it was like, or——"

"One moment, please. . . . Yes?"

"I saw another bottle with the same label this morning."

"You did? Where?"

"At Bales', the chemist's in Macebury."

"What were you doing at the chemist's this morning?"

"I ran my nephew into the town. He wanted to buy some papers, and then he saw the chemist's shop and said he wanted a nail-brush. He went inside, and I hung about outside. There were two or three of those bottles in the window."

"You didn't go into the shop yourself?"

"No."

"So you don't actually know that your nephew bought a nail-brush?"

"No, except that he came out with a white paper parcel which looked as if it had a nail-brush inside."

"Might the parcel have contained a bottle of this mixture, or of anything else?"

"I suppose so. But it was rather small, I think."

"Doesn't it seem to you rather extravagant, buying a nail-brush when you're only away for three nights? A nail-brush is an expensive article, isn't it?"

"You know as well as I do."

"I want your opinion, please."

51

"Yes, then."

"Is your nephew well off?"

"It depends what you mean. Considering he lives in London and has some smartish friends, perhaps he isn't."

"Is he extravagant?"

"I don't know. I suppose he spends pretty well all he has. Most young fellows do."

"Has he ever asked you for money?"

"Never. He knows I haven't any to spare."

"Or your wife?"

"I don't think so."

"You're not quite sure?"

"She never told me he had. I shouldn't think he would."

"Did Mrs. Cartwright care for him?"

"Yes, very much, I should say."

"Was he devoted to her?"

"Not devoted, perhaps. I never saw them getting on badly together. She seemed rather to admire him, and I'm sure she wouldn't have, if——"

"If what?"

"If they hadn't got on well together."

"Thank you. . . . I should like to know, sir, if you have any suspicions of any kind regarding the matter. You may speak with perfect freedom, and nothing you say will go any further without very good reasons."

"I have no suspicions."

"None at all?"

"None."

"Nothing has happened which has puzzled you?"

"Nothing, except, of course, the tragedy itself."

"Thank you. . . . As a matter of form, do you mind if I take your fingerprints?"

"I've no objection, though I don't see——"

"It's purely a routine business, sir. . . . Thank you. Now, Mr. Cartwright, I shall have to see all the servants—largely a matter of form. Will you kindly tell me who they are?"

"Dace, man-servant and chauffeur. Buxey, my wife's maid who also helps with the parlour-work. Ada—I don't know her other name—the housemaid. Mrs. Dury, the cook, and a kitchen-maid whose name I don't know. There are two gardeners, Smithwell and Capton, and a boy, Wrigley, who helps them and washes the car."

"How long have they been in service with you?"

"Buxey and Mrs. Dury at any rate before I married my wife. Oh, and the two gardeners too. Ada six months. Dace came in May last year. I engaged the boy Wrigley about four months ago. I know nothing about the kitchen-maid."

"Did you engage Dace?"

"No, my wife did."

"Have you anything to say about any of the servants?"

"No, they're a good lot. Dace is a bit off-hand, perhaps. Got a poor manner, you know. But he's a good driver, and I've had nothing special to complain of."

"Thank you. . . . Would you mind sending Dace up to me, please?"

"All right."

"Good morning, Mr. Cartwright."

I heard the door into the passage open and shut, and my uncle on his way downstairs. Then Glaize said, in a different voice, "Have a look at that nail-brush, Hare. . . . Oh, well, there's no great hurry. He'd have been a fool if he didn't buy one. Wait till I've finished with Dace."

There was a pause, and I looked across the room at my new nail-brush—my "expensive" nail-brush, which was lying in its paper wrapping on my dressing-table. So I was under suspicion? Under suspicion! The words seemed absurd. I suddenly felt restless, but was too eager to hear part of the interview with Dace to leave my post at once.

"Sit down, Dace. How long have you been in service here?"

"Since May last year, sir."

"Your duties are to drive the car, but not to clean it, and to act as butler-parlourman. Is that so?"

"Yes, sir."

"Have you been satisfied with your situation here?"

"Yes, sir, I've nothing to complain of."

"Nothing as regards Mr. Cartwright?"

"No, sir."

"You were engaged by Mrs. Cartwright?"

"Yes, sir—through an advertisement she put in the paper."

"Quite so. You have no duties upstairs?"

"No, sir, except valeting the gentlemen."

"When did you last come into this room?"

"During the spring-cleaning."

"And Mrs. Cartwright's bedroom?"

"On the same occasion."

"How did you first hear of your mistress's attack?"

Dace then corroborated my own account of what had happened. My attention wandered a little, but was recalled by hearing Glaize ask, "Did Mr. Warren tell you to get through to Mr. Cartwright?"

"Yes, sir. I tried to when I'd got the doctor, but there wasn't a reply."

"You tried to get Mr. Carvel's house and failed? Are you sure you were properly connected?"

"No, I can't be sure of that."

"You didn't try again?"

"No, sir."

"Why not?"

"I don't know. I had something else to do. It didn't seem important."

"Not important to let Mr. Cartwright know that his wife was so seriously ill? What do you mean? Do you imply that Mr. Cartwright was on such bad terms with his wife that it didn't matter to him whether she was at death's door or not?"

"No, I don't mean that exactly."

"But you thought the bad news would keep?"

"Yes. The main thing was to get on to the doctor."

"Of course it was, but after the doctor, Mr. Cartwright should have been told immediately, shouldn't he? Did you consider Mr. and Mrs. Cartwright very happy together?"

"I think they got a bit tired of one another sometimes."

"Did Mr. Cartwright give his wife any cause for jealousy?"

"Not that I know of."

"Very well, we may have to go back to this point later. Now tell me this. Did you know that your mistress had a bottle of a preparation called by a French name, 'Le Secret de Venus'?"

"No, sir."

"A pink bottle, rather like a flat scent bottle, with a shiny green label round the neck. Have you ever seen such a bottle?"

"No, not as far as I know."

"Did your mistress ever go to Bales', the chemist?"

"Yes, quite often."

"You used to drive her there?"

"Yes."

"When did you last drive her there?"

"On Friday morning before lunch—about a quarter to one, I should say."

"Did she go into the shop?"

"Yes."

"You didn't see what she was buying?"

"No, sir."

"Did she come out with a parcel?"

"Yes—or rather the shop assistant carried it out for her. It was a big parcel, and looked like three or four things done up together—lumpy-like, you know."

"Did she take the parcel home?"

"Yes, in the car. When we got home, I put it in the hall before I took the car round to the garage."

"Did you see the parcel again?"

"No. When I next passed through the hall, to sound the gong for lunch, it had gone."

55

"Thank you. Where do you sleep, Dace?"

"In the basement, at the back. Not exactly a proper basement, it isn't—the ground's cut away like, in front of it, making a kind of sunk yard."

"Did you hear any noises or notice anything suspicious during last night?"

"No, sir."

"Thank you. Well, I think that'll be . . ."

I did not wait to hear more, realising that as soon as Dace's finger-prints had been taken—I presumed that they would be—the search for my nail-brush would begin, and I had no wish to be discovered in my position, which I might some time care to use again. I got off my bed, therefore, straightened it as much as I could, to efface the impression of my body, by turning the eiderdown over, and was on the point of creeping out of the room, when I thought I heard steps on the landing. On the spur of the moment, I opened the door between my room and my uncle's, and went into the latter. To my relief, the door-handle made no sound.

For a few minutes, I remained, listening intently. I must have imagined the steps which had just startled me, but soon there were unmistakable sounds of someone going downstairs—probably Dace, and of someone else, probably Hare, going into my room. I thought I caught the chink of a tunic button against the handle of one of the drawers in the dressing-table. There was a noise of a door shutting softly, and all sounds ceased, till I heard more footsteps on the stairs—probably one of the servants arriving to be questioned. I gave the newcomer time to go into the boudoir, and went out diffidently into the passage, hoping not to be seen. I felt greatly comforted when I had reached the hall without meeting anyone on the way.

VIII

My Meditation

(Saturday, before Tea)

THE weather was "unsettled", and the reappearing sun
tempted me to a remote part of the garden. Besides, I wished
to be alone. At the risk of repeating myself, I must emphasise
the mental stress under which I was labouring. My impulse,
like the impulse of one who is suddenly beset by a grave
calamity, was to exclaim, "It is not real. I am dreaming",
and whenever my thoughts strayed from fact to fancy, as
they were often apt to do, I had, in recalling them, to give
battle to this scepticism.

Even as to the murder itself, my wits were wildly confused. My confidence that "truth would out" was ebbing.
I even began to wonder, like certain philosophers, whether
the word "truth" had any meaning, and to feel that of two
irreconcilables, each might in its way be real. "Here you
are," I told myself, "involved in a murder—you are under
suspicion. What are you going to do about it? Sit still and
smoke a cigarette?"

Yet if I was to "do anything about it" I was sadly unfitted
for the task. I had read a fair number of detective stories,
and could remember no hero who was not fearless, athletic,
and intuitive. I knew myself to be timid, physically clumsy,
and incapable of climbing up the side of a house, leaping
on to trains in motion, or wrestling with Alsatians. I distrusted intuition, and rarely acted from impulse—though,
when I did, my impulses were often fantastic. Hence, perhaps, my avoidance of them.

I was appalled too by the thought that every action which
I had performed and should perform during the next few
days, might, however trivial and irrelevant, play a part

in the drama. Witness my purchase of the nail-brush. I leave a nail-brush, almost worn-out, in London. I pass a chemist's shop in Macebury and buy a new one. What happens? Policemen break into my bedroom to search for it, as if for a blood-stained dagger, while I dart through a side door and creep about the house like a guilty ghost.

For some minutes my brain seethed so turbulently that I despaired of clearing it. Then it occurred to me that I might find a helpful discipline if I wrote down the subjects on which I wished to meditate. I would, I decided, go over each of these subjects in turn, and try to keep my thoughts from straying beyond it. The divisions between the subjects would be artificial, but I could break them down afterwards.

I still have the paper on which I wrote:

(1) Plain man or superior person?

(2) Motive.

(3) Alibi.

(4) Suspicion.

(5) My duty (!) and inclination.

(6) Agenda.

The result of my meditation, pruned of some extravagant offshoots, was as follows:

(1) *Plain man or superior person.*

Inspector Glaize is a plain man. So, presumably, are all the police, in spite of what I have read in some detective stories. These plain men have an excellent, though not perfect, organisation. They can trace telephone calls, have bits of fluff analysed, organise search parties, with small difficulty. They are expert in following the movements of people's bodies—much less expert in following the movements of people's minds.

The superior person approaches the problem from the opposite angle. He first says, "These things don't happen;"

later, "I was wrong. Let me think, and I will tell you the answer blindfold. I wish to see nothing, measure no footprints, hunt for no cigarette ends. My brain is my only microscope."

Which of the two shall I be? Clearly, a superior person. I use the word without pride, just as I say "plain man" without contempt. If I can, I will combine the two parts, but if they conflict. I will be "superior." In other words, I can't beat the police at their own game. I will not search for material clues.

Query: Am I really eager to find the murderer?
Answer: Postpone this till you come to (5).

Query: Then perhaps (5) ought to come next?
Answer: Don't begin rearranging your headings. Go straight on.

(2) *Motive.*

The motive is obviously money—eagerness to get it before due time, or fear of not getting it at all. (As a superior person, I refuse to believe that my aunt is the victim of a gang of international anarchists.)

Who may be influenced by this motive? All Aunt Catherine's relations and marriage-connections, in varying degrees. It is unlikely that Maria Hall's colonial children have as much interest in my aunt's will as Uncle Hannibal, Uncle Terence—or myself.

Do relations and marriage-connections complete the list of possibles? No. There might be someone with whom my aunt was on intimate terms, without our knowledge—a friend or a servant. We should probably have heard of an intimate friend. What about a servant? Dace? Buxey? Even a gardener? People do these things for very little, we are told. The hint of a ten-pound legacy might have been enough.

By the way, what of a homicidal maniac? Rubbish. Poison is not a maniac's weapon as a rule. At least, I don't think so.

(3) *Alibi.*

What does alibi mean? You have an alibi if you can prove that you were not on the spot when the crime was committed. But what is the commission of the crime in this case? Putting poison in the bottle, not offering the bottle to the victim. (This comes painfully near home.) To have an alibi, then, in this case, one must be able to show that one had no chance of getting at the bottle. A large order. What period does it cover? The period after the bottle reached this house, or after it reached Bales' in Macebury—if it was bought at Bales'—or after it was made in the factory? Probably the period after it reached this house—though the possibility of earlier tampering must not be ignored. Assuming this period to be the critical one, and assuming that the bottle was bought at Bales', who, amongst my chief suspects, have alibis, and who have not? Leave this for the next heading.

N.B.—Superior as I am, I must find out somehow if the bottle was bought at Bales' on Friday, as Dace's evidence suggested.

(4) *Suspicion.*

I suspect those: (*a*) with motive and (*b*) without alibi.

(*a*) The list is enormous.

(*b*) Who have complete alibis? (i) My mother, my sisters, my brother-in-law, my stepfather. (ii) Uncle Terence and the Teirsons. (iii) Aunt Fanny. (iv) (Probably) all Maria Hall's children. It is, of course, possible that any of these people could have paid a clandestine visit to Macebury, by travelling there and back at great speed, but it seems unlikely. As for Uncle Terence, if he is where he purports to be, I daresay nothing but an aeroplane could have brought him here in time. I ought to examine this more carefully, but I cannot seriously think that the poison was put in the bottle by any long-distance traveller. How should such a person know that Aunt Catherine had bought the bottle? She kept the purchase secret, and even if she did write to someone of it, in confidence, the letter could not have reached anyone at a distance till this morning. Might she have telegraphed about it? Rubbish.

And now, who have partial alibis? By this, I mean those who, while physically able to enter Otho House after the bottle's arrival, must have done so secretly, if they did.

To answer this, I should, I suppose, question all the servants and my uncle. I have the impression, from what my uncle told me, that my aunt's movements during the past thirty hours have been very simple. I assume she bought the bottle before luncheon on Friday, and brought it back wrapped up in a large parcel. She had luncheon, and went to her room to rest. She had tea alone downstairs, but did not leave the garden, even if she went into it. She dined in her boudoir and went to bed.

I have my uncle's word—which should be tested—that no visitors arrived after six o'clock yesterday, when he came back from whatever he was doing in the country. For the moment, I ignore the time during which he was meeting me, and the time we spent in Macebury this morning. Any persons, therefore, with partial alibis, whose movements I can account for between three and six yesterday afternoon, may be given almost complete alibis.

Are there any such? Most probably Bob Carvel and the brothers Dennis who would have been at their office. And of course Anne Carvel and Muriel, who went to London at 11.40 and did not return till the evening—or so I am led to believe.

At this point I felt in my pocket and found a crumpled company prospectus. The last page was nearly blank, and left me room to draw up the following table. I remembered enjoying a similar table in a book by Lynn Brock, and saw no reason why I should not adopt the method. After all, most people (superior or plain), when confronted with a case of murder, have little but their knowledge of detective stories to guide them. Certainly I had little else, for I did not read newspaper reports of criminal trials.

SUSPECTS

(Omitting those with absolutely complete alibis)

Name	Motive	Weakness of Alibi	Opportunity	Murderous Disposition	Total
Maximum marks	10	10	10	10	40
Hannibal Cartwright	10	10	10	1	31
Dace	3	10	7	1	21
Buxey	3	10	9	0	22
Other indoor servants	2	10	7–4	0?	19–16
Outdoor servants	2	5	3	0?	10
Myself	10	10	10	1	31
Anne Carvel/Muriel Carvel	3	2	1	0	6
Bob Carvel	8	4	3	0	15
Henrietta Carvel	3	5	3	0	11
The Brothers Dennis	5	4	3	?	12
Elizabeth Dennis	3	5	3	0	11
Mary Dennis	1	5	3	?	9
Maria Hall	3	5	3	10	21

In assigning these marks, I tended to assume that in Aunt Catherine's will, males would be preferred to females. Had my sisters been on the list, I should have given them fewer marks for motive than I gave myself. Compare Bob Carvel's marks with those of his sisters. The Dennis brothers received 5, because it would have been foolish of them to expect too much. Terence Carvel, had he appeared, would have had 10, Bob with a father living, seemed less favourably placed than I with a mother. The marks for murderous disposition were something of a joke, and it was only spite that made me give Maria Hall the maximum. I have met her once—a fat, garrulous, Rembrandtesque figure—and disliked her. Still she had telephoned on Friday night. Why? Was it solicitude or infamous curiosity?

Even at the time, I was not very proud of my table. It was built up on suppositions which were still unproven. The more I considered my marking, the more arbitrary it seemed. The way of the superior person is hard. Yet I felt that even those plain men, the police, would have agreed with the beginning of my order—equal first, Uncle Hannibal and myself, then Buxey, then equal Dace and Maria Hall. As to Maria Hall, they did not know of her telephone call or murderous disposition. I began myself to take her quite seriously. Had it been a detective story, she would have had my vote, as not too obvious but obvious enough.

(5) *My duty and inclination.*

I do not believe that poor Aunt Catherine's blood is crying out for vengeance, or that there is a moral law, erect as a spiritual Eiffel Tower, which compels all citizens to do their best to hand over all murderers to the state.

I do not believe that the state has a "right" to punish the murderer, though no doubt it is usually expedient that it should do so.

I do not believe that murder is always the most awful of all sins. It may not even be a sin at all.

I do not believe in retributive punishment.

I am not inclined to hand anyone over to "justice."

I am not inclined to do dirty work for the police.

But I should not be terribly distressed if some of my relations (Uncle Terence, for example) were taken away quietly and executed.

I know I should have, despite my theories, a revulsion from the society of a murderer. Though capable of concealing the truth, I find it hard to tell a direct lie even in a good cause. I do not think I could bring myself to work against the police. Besides, it would be dangerous for me.

Suppose Uncle Hannibal is the murderer, what shall I do? Suppose I know things about him which the police do not know? My inclination is, in a negative way, to save him. But is it my duty, or my inclination, to make myself liable to imprisonment as accessory after the fact? Yet I should be very sorry to be the means of his conviction.

A new point. If the right murderer is not found, may the police not find the wrong one? What about me? Of course, this is unthinkable.

Again I seem to remember that a murderer often covers his traces by another murder—especially if he thinks someone knows too much. Suppose Uncle Hannibal is the murderer, am I very safe here? For these two reasons, it is greatly to my interest that the real murderer should quickly be found.

If I could find the murderer myself, I should know better what I want to do. If I rush to the police with any clues I may think I have, I may bring an innocent person into danger. A horrible responsibility.

I wish to solve this mystery myself. Upon the answer, my subsequent conduct will depend.

(6) *Agenda.*

(i) Find out if the bottle was bought at Bales' by Aunt Catherine yesterday morning, shortly before luncheon.

(ii) Find out, tactfully, whether Aunt Catherine is known to have had any visitors between luncheon yesterday and my visit to her room this morning.

(iii) Find out whether it would have been easy for any visitor to come in unobserved during this period.

(iv) Find out as much police evidence as possible, particularly as to finger-marks on bottle or desk. Eavesdrop if necessary.

(v) Search for domestic scandals.

(vi) Consider every event which, since my arrival, seems now to have been in the slightest degree unusual. Try to form a sequence between such events, and interpret them.

(vii) Go in. It's starting to rain.

IX

Tea

(Saturday)

I WENT into the house by the front door. The drawing-room door was open, and I saw my uncle standing in front of the bookcase, his hands in his pockets. Tea was set out on a table.

As I shut the drawing-room door, my uncle turned round.

"Are they still here?" I asked.

"Some of them."

I sighed, and sat in an armchair by the table.

"I wonder what they're doing."

"Don't know. Help yourself, will you?"

As I ate, he strolled moodily round the room.

"I've been wondering—" I said weakly.

"What about?"

"Whether Aunt Catherine had any visitors since luncheon yesterday."

"She hadn't any."

"But you weren't in all the afternoon, were you?"

"No. I had a round of golf. But I asked Buxey, who was in all day. No one called. Better leave this kind of thing to the police to sort out. We've enough to think of as it is. These have come."

He gave me two telegrams, one from my mother and one from Aunt Fanny. Both contained conventional words of sympathy, and Aunt Fanny's ended, "Ought I to come?"

"I must put Aunt Fanny off," I said.

"Yes."

"And, Uncle Hannibal, we ought to get a solicitor here as soon as we can, I think."

"Bob Carvel's the man for that. Did you gather when he would be here?"

"Aunt Anne was going to send for him. But in the meantime, I suppose Luke and Harry Dennis are somewhere about. Ought we to try to get on to them?"

"Oh, let's leave it till Bob comes."

I poured out another cup of tea. I was a little distressed at my uncle's gruffness, and felt that he might have apologised for involving me in such a joyless week-end. I began to think of the next two days with dismay. Meanwhile, I had to send another telegram to Aunt Fanny, urging her to stay in London. I was preparing in my mind the wording of it, when Dace came in to say that Inspector Glaize wished to see me in the boudoir. I looked at my uncle, but he made no comment. "Is it possible," I wondered, as I went upstairs, "that I am going to be arrested?" When I confronted Glaize, I was red in the face and very nervous. Another man in plain clothes was with him. Glaize was perhaps more affable than he had been before.

"I'm sorry to trouble you again, Mr. Warren," he said, after telling me to sit down, "but I must ask you a few more questions. It's about the bottle. I want you to go through the exact motions you went through this morning, when you looked for the blotting-paper. Let me arrange things as they were, first. The blotter was lying flat in the bureau, wasn't it, like this?"

"Yes."

"The investment book wasn't in the bureau, of course?"

"No."

"And where shall I put the bottle? We'll use this bottle of Eno's Fruit Salts instead of the real bottle, if you don't mind. Here?"

"I think so. I'm not sure of the exact position."

"I want you to be as sure of everything as you can. Was it here?"

"Yes—rather to the left, I daresay."

"Here?"

"Yes."

"Very well. I'm going to shut the bureau. You can imagine you've just unlocked it. I want you to do just what you did this morning, but dead slow—like those films you see sometimes. I may interrupt you, and if I say 'Stop', I want you to remain exactly as you are, without moving. Are you ready? Go."

Very gingerly I opened the bureau, stared at the bottle while I counted sixty, and then lifted it up slowly so as to put it on the top of the bureau.

"Stop."

I stopped, and the Inspector came close up to me and stared at my hand which held the bottle.

"You're sure you held it like this?"

"I can't swear to it, but I think——"

"All right. Go on."

I laid the bottle on the bureau, opened the blotter, took out two sheets of blotting-paper, shut the bureau again and pretended to lock it. I then turned away from the bureau, took two very deliberate paces towards my aunt's door, paused, turned round again and went back to the bureau. After another pause, I transferred the blotting-paper to my left hand and picked up the bottle with my right.

"Stop."

I stopped.

"Go on."

I walked to the door leading into my aunt's bedroom.

"That door was open," I said.

"Turn round. Now you must imagine that this is Mrs. Cartwright's bedroom. This sofa is the bed, and if you'll excuse me, I'll act the part of Mrs. Cartwright. It was the left side of the bed you approached, wasn't it?"

"Yes. My aunt was leaning over on her left side, so as to be able to use the sofa-table."

"I shall want you to tell me what to do, in a minute. You needn't bother with what was said. Wait a bit."

67

The Inspector placed himself awkwardly on a sofa which stood against the landing wall.

"Mrs. Cartwright would have her right hand quite free?"

"Oh yes. I think she would be leaning on her left elbow."

"All right. Go on."

Slowly I went up to the Inspector, and held out the blotting-paper with my left hand.

"You take this," I said, "and put it down somewhere—on the sofa-table, I think."

With little ceremony, he took the blotting-paper and dropped it on the floor.

"Go on. Very slowly, please."

Tantalisingly I held the bottle up in my right hand.

"You stretch your hand out," I said, "almost as if you wanted to grab it."

"Like this?"

"Yes; you're stretching over the sofa-table, remember."

"About here?"

"Yes."

I lowered the bottle.

"Now you take it."

"Stop. Tell me exactly how I'm to take it. Do I force your hand open? Do I touch your hand at all?"

"I don't think so. You take the bottle by the neck. Perhaps your fingers touch my thumb and my forefinger. I'm really not very sure. . . ."

"Please be as sure as you can."

"Well, if you do touch my fingers, you only just graze them. You snatch at the bottle neck."

"All right."

He pounced at the neck and I released the bottle, leaving it in his fat fingers.

"Was it like this?"

"Yes, but not so violently. The action was more playful, and—er—delicate."

He grinned.

"Well, we'll take that for granted. You let the bottle go, like you did just now?"

"Yes."

"Now, what do I do?"

"You take out the stopper."

"How do I hold the bottle? In which hand?"

"I really don't know. I'm very sorry, but I have no recollection of this part. All I know is, you take out the stopper put the bottle on the table for a moment, pour some hot water into the tumbler, and empty some crystals from the bottle into it. If you do it as it comes naturally, I dare say it will be the right way."

The Inspector swung his feet to the floor.

"Well, this part isn't very important, as a matter of fact. I do take the bottle fair and square in my hand, I suppose? I don't hold it by the neck the whole time?"

"I don't think so. I am sure you don't."

"So am I," he said mysteriously, and getting off the sofa, he beckoned to his companion. a small man with a red face and white moustache, who had been watching our mummery in silence. Together they went to the window.

I sat down on the sofa.

"Quite obviously they'll be there," I heard the unknown say, after a few moments' muttering. "All over the shop. . . ."

The word "shop" struck a responsive chord in me.

"Excuse me." I said.

Glaize turned round.

"Well?"

"I wonder if you'll mind my asking you a question?"

"I don't mind you asking, though I don't guarantee to answer it. Fire away."

"Is there anything to show when the bottle first came into my aunt's possession?"

Glaize looked at me with a solemn frown, pursed his lips, and said:

"Well, I see no harm in giving you an answer to that, especially as you've just been so obliging and I hope will oblige me again. Mrs. Cartwright bought the bottle containing the mixture at Bales', the chemist's shop in Macebury, at twelve minutes to one yesterday."

"Oh!" I felt I ought to compliment him on his discovery, and also that my question needed an explanation, however feeble.

"I heard this gentleman," I continued, "mention the word 'shop' just now, and I wondered if you knew in what shop the bottle was——"

At this both the men laughed.

"Oh, I see," said Glaize. "All over the shop. That didn't mean quite what you thought, Mr. Warren. It meant all over something else—all over the bottle, in fact. Rather a more difficult matter, too, than tracing the purchase to Bales'."

"Perhaps," I suggested, "I could help you, if you told me exactly what you're getting at."

Glaize hesitated, and then said, "I dare say you'd get at it yourself, if you thought over what you've just been doing. But first I'm going to warn you not to pass on to anyone at all anything you may learn while you're—collab'rating with us, I might call it. What we're puzzled by is this. When you handled the bottle just now, you made finger-marks all over it—all over the shop—except perhaps within an inch or two of the neck. You made prints on the blotting-paper you used just now, and on the blotting-paper you took to Mrs. Cartwright this morning. That shows you weren't wearing gloves then. But this is the snag. On the bottle containing the mixture, we haven't found any trace of your finger-marks at all. We've found Mrs. Cartwright's, on the stopper and neck and lower down, but not one of yours. That's the little problem we're tackling now. Can you explain it?"

I pondered for a moment, and then, forgetting that I had decided not to blurt out everything to the police, stood up excitedly and said, "I've got it. I never touched the bottle containing the mixture at all!"

They stared at me in amazement, and I continued.

"There was a paper wrapper round the bottle, covering all the lower part. I should think it went to within an inch and a half of the neck. It was wrapped tightly round, and, of course, it was that that I touched."

"Good Lord! To think we didn't——What became of this wrapper?"

"When my aunt took the bottle by the neck, it slipped out of the wrapper, which remained in my hand. I read the wrapper after she took the first sip."

The men looked at one another in consternation.

"You didn't mention reading it when you told your story," said Glaize suspiciously.

"Didn't I? Are you sure?"

He took out a notebook.

"What you said was this: 'My aunt poured some crystals rather like Epsom salts, into the tumbler. She said, "I'm going to finish my letter." I sat down while she did so. After a short time, perhaps five minutes, I looked up and she raised the tumbler to her lips. She said, "What a bitter taste!"' Then comes the French. 'She smiled and lay down and shut her eyes. I remained seated in my chair. Suddenly I was appalled to hear my aunt moan loudly'—and so on. Not a word about the wrapper."

"I'm afraid I must have been too upset to think of it. I'm very sorry."

"I should think so. Of course, Mr. Warren, we quite understand that you didn't realise the importance of the wrapper at the time, but it may be a very important matter indeed to us."

"Perhaps, if you'd asked me what I was doing while I was sitting down . . ." I suggested in self-defence.

He murmured something which I did not catch, and continued, "Well, what became of the wrapper, anyhow? Can you remember that?"

"I—yes. I must have stuffed it in my pocket, because I

pulled it out in the drawing-room while waiting for Dr. Bradford, and threw it into the fireplace."

"Into the fire?"

"No. The fire wasn't lit. Into the fender."

"Crumpled up?"

"I think so."

"Did you mention the wrapper to Dr. Bradford?"

"No, I don't think so."

"Did you mention it to——Never mind that now, though. For all you know, is the wrapper still in the drawing-room fender?"

"Yes—for all I know."

"Then, by God, if it is, we'll have it."

At that, he opened the door to the landing, pushed me through it, followed me out with his companion, locked the door, and hurried past me down the stairs. When I reached the drawing-room, he was searching the fireplace.

"Is it there?" I asked.

Clearly it was not, or he was pretending that it was not. He looked up at me with his moon of a face.

"That's all, Mr. Warren, thank you, for the time being."

Through the window, I could see my uncle and my Aunt Anne, walking together on the lawn. I went through the French window leading on to the terrace, and joined them.

X

A Walk with Aunt Anne

(*Saturday, after tea*)

ANNE CARVEL was my only relative—if I may include connections by marriage in the term—who had ever heard of Pirandello, Bela Bartok, and Utrillo. If she had not married Uncle Terence, she might have painted, written novels, or designed ballets. As a child, before I could realise that we had some tastes in common. I took a dislike to her, and the lack of enthusiasm which our branch of the family had always felt for the male Carvels, made me slow to know her better, when my judgment developed. None the less, I used to feel relieved when she came to tea at Otho House, especially if she came without husband or children. She was dark and palely beautiful. She had horrified my mother and my aunts by being shingled early. Uncle Terence was very proud of her—or so we said. Bob was devoted to her. She was devoted to Bob. There was perhaps an absence of sympathy between her and her daughters.

Aunt Catherine was forced to admire her. She was so clearly more interesting and accomplished than Aunt Catherine's other female dependents—Elizabeth Dennis, Maria Hall, and Mrs. Harry Dennis, the solicitor's wife. She could be useful, and was no doubt paid for her services. I suspect it was she who helped my aunt to redecorate her bedroom and boudoir, even though it must have been an effort for Aunt Catherine to seek her advice.

I knew little of the cross-currents of domestic affection in the family at that time, but I had begun to conjecture—whenever I thought about such matters—that Uncle Terence's "pride" in his wife was a thin emotion. If Aunt Anne had been of more resolute character, she would either have ruled in her own house or left it. As it was, she compromised by trying to find congenial friends in Macebury, which was hard, and by attaching herself to Otho House. She had, I think, a more generous nature than the Carvels, and was less disposed to criticise Aunt Catherine's second marriage. Hence, favour with Aunt Catherine and gratitude from Uncle Hannibal, from whom she differed in almost every possible way.

"I am so very sorry about all this," she said when I came up. "I mean, for you now as well as what happened this morning. Hannibal tells me that these people are still keeping the whole house on tenterhooks. I suppose they must, but somehow—it forces one to look at things with such a narrow field of vision, just at a time when—one wants space for one's emotions."

Her style of speaking was perhaps a little borrowed from one of Elizabeth Bibesco's novels, but her sentences gave me time to readjust myself to rational society.

"I've just had my second 'interrogation'," I said. "You must excuse me if I seem very stupid."

At the time, I was thinking, "How difficult it is to meet someone after the death of a mutual friend, as a rule, and how easy she's made it."

"D'you think they want me, now?" my uncle asked.

"They didn't say so. They're conducting a kind of search-party."

"What on earth for?"

"Oh, finger-prints."

"I'd better go, I think. Well, good-bye, Anne. I know Malcolm's grateful to you for coming to see him. Perhaps they'll let him see you home. I'll have a word with the Inspector."

He went back to the house.

"I've telegraphed to Terence," she said, "but there hasn't been any answer yet. I don't suppose he'll get it till late to-night. Probably he'll be here by tomorrow afternoon. You'll be glad to have somebody who knows about the

74

practical side of these terrible affairs. I wired to Bob, too, and I should think he'll catch a train to-night. I'll send him round to you before luncheon to-morrow, unless you feel you'd rather see no one in the morning. And now I want to know about your sister."

I gave such news as I had, and for a while, as we strolled up and down the lawn, our talk was general. After about twenty minutes, she said she must be going home, and I said I would escort her if the police allowed it. There was a constable on duty by the gate, but I thought it better to ask Glaize himself for permission. Besides, I might be able to glean some more information from him. Aunt Anne waited in the drive while I went indoors. I found Glaize and his companion in the little smoking-room on the ground floor, and made my request.

"All right," he said. "Mr. Cartwright told me you might be wanting to go out, and I've left word with Robbins by the gate. If you're not back in two hours, we'll hunt for you!"

"Have you found the wrapper?" I asked.

"I should rather not disclose that, at present, Mr. Warren."

"Very well. Thank you for letting me go."

I walked out, I hope, with dignity. The betting, I thought, was five to one that they had not found the wrapper. If I was right, there was another puzzle for me to solve. How had it disappeared? It should have been in a wastepaper-basket or dust-bin, even if Dace had done his work properly, and tidied up the drawing-room.

I overtook Aunt Anne near the gate leading into the road. The policeman saluted as we passed. For the first part of our walk we avoided the subject of the murder, until it became clear that our thoughts were still busy with it.

"It's no use," said my aunt, "I must ask you a few things. Hannibal told me the outline—how the poison was taken and when the bottle was bought. . . ."

"When the bottle was bought?"

"Yes. Didn't you gather that? Catherine bought it yesterday morning at Bales' in Macebury. I didn't know there was any secret about that. Besides, she told me she was going to get it."

"She told you? This may be terribly important, Aunt Anne. I'm not sure that we oughtn't to go back to the police at once. If you really have a 'story'——"

She made a gesture of distaste.

"I shall leave you to judge," she said, "what I ought to do. The bit I know isn't in the least bit sinister or mysterious. I went to see Catherine on Friday morning—before I went to London with Muriel. Catherine, of course, was still in bed. She saw I wasn't looking well—in fact, she knew I was worried about my health—and she told me, with just a touch of *pudeur* perhaps, about this quack mixture. She'd heard about it—I forget from whom. I asked if I should bring her back some from London, but she said she remembered seeing it at Bales', and might get a bottle that morning when she went into the town. I think she really may have got it for me."

"So you knew the stuff was in the house last night? Do you realise you are the only person who knew this?"

"I may be—the only person except one. I suppose there was someone, last night or this morning, who knew—and used his knowledge."

"How did Uncle Hannibal know about the stuff being bought at Bales'?"

"I'm not sure. It seemed natural to me that he should know. When he told me how the poison was given, I said, 'That's what poor Catherine was urging me to take.' Perhaps he knew she'd been to Bales' on Friday—she or Dace may have told him that—and assumed that she had bought the stuff then."

"How do you think he's affected by things?" I asked.

"He's simply numb with shock and surprise. It would be silly to pretend that he was violently in love with Catherine. You look at these things as I do, Malcolm, and there's no need for us to be too conventional about them when we're alone. Hannibal is dazed. He doesn't know what to do, or whom he can rely on. He's frightened. Malcolm, how far do they suspect him?"

"About as far as they suspect me, I think. We both had splendid chances of doing it. As long as there are two of us under a cloud, I don't think they'll be in a hurry to arrest either. When one is cleared—but I don't see how either of us can be cleared till the murderer is caught. As long as the murderer is unknown, Uncle Hannibal and I are the chief suspects."

She took my hand, and her eyes filled with tears.

"Oh, Malcolm. . . ."

"Don't worry about me," I said. "The consciousness of innocence is a great comfort. I simply can't believe that a mistake will be made. It's true there's nothing but my word to show that I didn't put the poison in the bottle, but as I didn't do it, there can't be any evidence to show that I did—unless, of course, the evidence is forged. But this seems a little too melodramatic. I'm still sane enough to judge things by the standards of everyday life and not by Edgar Wallace."

"It couldn't have been suicide?"

"I suppose it's physically possible that Aunt Catherine put the poison in the bottle herself, but everything else points the other way."

"Yes, it does."

We had now reached the Carvels' house. "Come in for a moment, won't you?" she said. "There's nobody about."

"Where are Muriel and Henrietta?"

She smiled.

"You needn't be so frightened of them. They're probably sitting in the tent in the garden at the back. We won't look for them."

She led the way to her own sitting-room, a converted conservatory at the side of the house. It was much more a studio than a boudoir. She had always had a fondness for "arts and crafts," and amused herself by modelling little figures, binding books and carving. We sat down on a broad divan covered with a multitude of cushions.

"Now," she said. "Ought I to go to the police?"

"Yes. Not because your story adds to what they already know—I don't think it does—but because it might look strange afterwards if you didn't go. They will ask you innumerable questions."

She sighed.

"What questions?"

"Amongst others, whether you are quite sure you didn't go to Bales' instead of Aunt Catherine or before Aunt Catherine, whether you visited Otho House after you came back from London, exactly when you came back from London, exactly what Aunt Catherine said to you about the mixture —oh, and other questions about my and Uncle Hannibal's relations with Aunt Catherine."

"It'll be tedious, I see. It's the last question I don't quite like. I suppose they imagine that all proper husbands dote on their wives. It'll be difficult—or impossible to make them understand."

"Simply say that as far as you know, Uncle Hannibal and Aunt Catherine always got on very well together."

"Yes. Did they ask you about that?"

"Yes. When I tried to give a rational answer, it was suggested that I took a cynical view of marriage. What about the other questions?"

She looked for a moment slightly surprised that I referred to them, and then replied with a trace of formality in her voice:

"On leaving Mrs. Cartwright, I went straight home, picked up my daughter Muriel and drove to the station, where I caught the 11.20 for London. I remained in London till, with my daughter, I caught the train leaving King's Cross at 6.21. The train arrived at Macebury at 7.48. The car met us, and we drove straight home. I went upstairs to dress, and at 8.15 dined with my two daughters and my son. We sat

78

together till about half-past nine, when I went to bed. I did not leave this house at all till I walked over to Otho House this afternoon. Will that do?"

"Yes, very well. Of course they'll want to corroborate all you say. They may want to see Muriel and your chauffeur. They may go to Bales' and find out if you called there. I'm only warning you what they're like."

"Poor Malcolm. I don't mind. They can see Muriel and West and go to Bales'. There's no difficulty there. What I am upset about is—you and Hannibal."

"Does Uncle Hannibal suspect me?"

"Of course not. Do you, Malcolm, suspect him at all?"

She looked at me searchingly and I blushed.

"I can understand the police suspecting him."

"Yes, but—you?"

"I don't know why I should be on the defensive with you," I said. "In some ways, I can't help suspecting him."

At this, she burst into tears. I got up and walked with embarrassment round the room.

In a minute or two, she said in her normal voice, "Forgive me, Malcolm. I don't know why I did that. I suppose I'm more affected than I thought I was. You will, as long as you can, keep an open mind, won't you?"

"Of course. I don't want to sus——I mean, I'm fond of him. Aunt Anne, is everything all right with you?"

I stood in front of her, and she met my look without flinching.

"You mean, about my visit to the doctor on Friday?"

"Yes."

"I think so. I hope so. I get very nervous about myself sometimes, and had rather a paroxysm lately. I think it'll pass off all right. I've often imagined things before. I want to show you your Christmas present."

"My Christmas present?"

She got up, and I followed her to a deal table.

"I was doing this for you," she said, and held up a grey morocco binding.

79

"How lovely, and how very kind of you."

"I intended it for Regnier's *La Pécheresse*. Do you know the book?"

"Yes, I love it."

"I'm so glad."

"I enjoyed it more than any novel I've read in the last twelve months. How well you know my tastes. I shall long for Christmas." I paused, and added, hoping the transition was not too abrupt, "I think I ought to go now. Shall I tell the Inspector to call on you?"

"If you think fit."

"I will, then. Good-bye."

As we shook hands, she smiled.

I walked back to Otho House, went up to my bedroom and lay down. There were no sounds of voices from the boudoir.

XI

Saturday Evening

DURING my walk back to Otho House, I had for the first time during my visit been overwhelmed with hopeless depression. I yearned to be away, leading my usual life—no longer because I resented being plunged into the sanctimonious atmosphere of death, but because I felt miserable and sad. I found it hard to say why, but since my meeting with Aunt Anne, my mood, instead of being dry, self-centred, and intellectualistic, had become fluid, sympathetic, and sentimental.

Yet, since my meditation in the garden, I had learnt much. The problem was not at rest but in motion. In grappling with it, speed was essential.

I had, when I lay down, to consider the following new facts—first that the wrapper had disappeared, secondly, though this seemed unimportant to me, that Aunt Anne, and almost certainly Muriel, had complete alibis, thirdly, that Uncle Hannibal knew when the bottle was bought, and, most important of all, that Aunt Anne was in love with Uncle Hannibal. She might, I reflected, have to be protected against herself. How far did he know of the infatuation, and respond to it? How far did he presume on it? And had Aunt Catherine known?

I had seen no signs of the police on my way upstairs, and decided to tell my uncle that I thought they ought to see Aunt Anne, before putting them in touch with her. Not only would my uncle think me less officious if I spoke to him first, but I should have a chance of seeing how he took my news. At this point, I fell asleep.

Uncle Hannibal awakened me at a quarter to eight. Dinner

was ready. I undid my nail brush (which, though I could tell it had been unwrapped, had been made into a neat parcel by Hare) and washed. A dismal meal followed. No detective story that I can remember lays sufficient stress on the horror of meals after a murder. I began to count those ahead of me. Sunday breakfast, luncheon, tea, and supper. Monday breakfast, luncheon——. Surely something would happen by then.

After dinner we had tepid coffee in the drawing-room. Without much preamble, I told Uncle Hannibal what Aunt Anne had said to me. He agreed that she must see the police, and said he would mention it to them the next day.

"Are they coming to-morrow?" I asked.

"You bet they will."

"When you left Aunt Anne after tea, what were they doing?"

"Rushing about the house like a pack of bloodhounds. I'm sick of it all. I don't want to sound unfeelin', but it's more than a man can stand. I don't know what to do. I don't know whether I'm master in my house or not. It isn't my own house, anyhow."

"Is there any way in which I can help you?"

"No. Malcolm, thank you. You've been awfully decent about things, and I'm glad, for my sake, to have you here. Not for yours, though. If you'll excuse me, I'll lock up and turn in. You won't be going outside again, will you?"

"No, it's too cold."

"Well, there's whisky in the dining-room."

"Thanks very much."

"Good-night, then."

At the door he paused.

"You don't feel scared of sleeping here, do you? Some people might be upset rather, in a house where a——"

"Oh no. I shall be quite all right. What time is breakfast to-morrow?"

"Half-past nine'll do. Dace will call you. At least he's supposed to. Good-night."

82

When he had gone upstairs, I fetched the whisky, and settling myself at the desk in the drawing-room, tried to make headway with the sixth point in my "agenda."

Events which since my arrival (and before) seem to have been in the slightest degree unusual.

1. I was sent for at very short notice.
2. The telegram was sent to my home address, not to the office, making it impossible for me to arrive early.
3. Maria Hall's telephone call.
4. My peculiar instructions regarding the investment book.
5. I am given the small bedroom next to the boudoir, instead of the spare room.
6. My bed has only one blanket.
7. I awoke in the night and saw light coming through the keyhole in the door between my room and my uncle's.
8. My uncle's early morning visit to me, and his interest in my bath.
9. When I get up, I find the key of the bureau lying on my handkerchief, and not underneath it.
10. Uncle Hannibal's whereabouts are vague during my interview with my aunt.
11. I do not remember noticing the bottle when I went to the bureau on Friday night. On Saturday morning it attracted my attention at once.
12. Uncle Hannibal knew about the purchase of the bottle at Bales'.
13. He was able to describe it accurately to Glaize, though he had only caught a glimpse of it when in my aunt's bedroom with Doctor Bradford. When Glaize foolishly showed surprise, H. corrected himself by saying that he had seen similar bottles at Bales'.
14. I pointed out the wrapper to my uncle, while it was in the drawing-room fender. Later, the wrapper has disappeared.

XII

Sunday Morning, Afternoon, and Evening

(i) Morning

I GROUP Sunday morning, afternoon, and evening together, not only because the day was one of fewer incidents than Saturday, but also because my own feelings, instead of fluctuating as they had done before, preserved the same quality throughout, though every hour they grew more intense. Except for two visits which I shall describe, there was nothing to distract me from my thoughts. The day, taken as a whole, was unbearably long. I awoke early, about six, and could not go to sleep again. About seven I got up and had my bath, and spent over an hour walking briskly in the garden. It was cold and the weather promised more wind and showers.

I met my uncle at breakfast. We said nothing that was at all important. He seemed to find it almost impossible to talk to me. The Sunday papers arrived, and I looked at them with apprehension. They contained no mention of the murder. My uncle went to the garage to work on his motor-bicycle. "He spends his time in the garage," Terence Carvel had once said, "because he feels most at home there." I sat down at the piano in the drawing-room, and played some Handel suites, hoping that the servants would take them for "sacred" music. They would never have approved of Beethoven.

I played badly and carelessly, and went out into the garden again. At about half-past eleven, I saw my cousin Bob Carvel coming through the gates. I had dreaded the meeting with him, as I now dreaded meetings with every new-comer. Besides, I never really enjoyed being with him.

He came up to me jauntily, though not without nervousness. We shook hands.

"So poor old Catherine's gone," he said, and then added. "A beastly business. Malcolm. We shall have to get to the bottom of it."

"It's a very difficult and unpleasant situation for us here," I said. "I've been wanting a solicitor to come. I suppose you know what to do?"

"The first thing, in a case of this kind," he answered, "is to get hold of the will. I got Luke Dennis on the 'phone and consulted him. Of course, you know we acted for Aunt Catherine in most things. But we didn't make her will. All parties preferred that we shouldn't. We sent her for that to a little man called Smoult—quite an able fellow in a small way. That was the time of Aunt Catherine's marriage to the man Cartwright. I've been round to Smoult's house this morning, and he told me a good deal. Mind, I oughtn't to be talking like this to you, but as things will come out in a day or two, I don't see the harm in it. I trust you to keep your mouth shut in the meantime, and not to let me down."

"Of course."

"Catherine made her first will—or rather I mean her first will after Cartwright came on the scene, a few days before her marriage. I gather Cartwright was the principal beneficiary. But this will was revoked and torn up about eight months ago, when Catherine made another, under which Cartwright got rather less. In April, she made a third will, and this is the effective one."

"Can you disclose the terms of it?" I asked, with a blush.

"I can, roughly. Smoult had a note of them at his house. The actual will, of course, is in the safe at his office. You and I are the executors—and it may interest you to know that we get a thousand pounds each for our trouble. To come to the main items, after a whole host of little legacies—green vase to Mabel, pink photo-frame to Phyllis kind of idea, you know—the money is divided into six unequal shares. One share, ten-fortieths of the residue, goes bang to charity, religious institutions, hospitals, and what not. Another share, six-fortieths, goes to the Dennises, partly on trust and partly outright. Third share, eight-fortieths, goes to my branch—father first, for life, then half to me outright and half for my sisters, with trusts. Your mother gets another eight-fortieths for life, two-thirds of which come to you on her death, while your sisters get the other third on trusts. Fifth share, seven-fortieths, to Aunt Fanny for life, and on her death, if no children—and of course there won't be any—as to three-elevenths to the Dennis fund, four-elevenths to the Terence Carvel fund, and four-elevenths to the Clara Oldmarsh fund —your mother's."

"What extraordinary figures."

"Not at all. They simply preserve the proportions of six-fortieths, eight-fortieths, and eight-fortieths, which those funds take in the residue to begin with. Of course there are all kinds of other provisions, trying to provide for deaths in a peculiar order. But as far as you and I are concerned, we've got definite vested interests in our shares of our respective funds. That's to say, if you survive your mother, you're bound to come into two-thirds of her fund absolutely, and even if you die before her, you can leave the reversion of it as you like by will—or assign it by deed—which means you can borrow on the strength of it, or sell it. Laymen don't generally understand these things. They're apt to think if they don't get the money outright, they've got to wait for the death of the one who has the life-interest before they can do anything. That's not so at all, unless the gift is contingent on their surviving the life tenant. And in our cases, it isn't."

"I think I follow."

"Well, that's five shares. The sixth share, as simple arithmetic will tell you, is one-fortieth. $10+6+8+8+7=39$. This one-fortieth goes outright to the man Cartwright. I haven't any idea what the old lady was really worth, but I should think, from what I know of the Dennis estate, that the residue, after payment of legacies and duties, would be worth between three hundred and four hundred thousand pounds. That's to say, Cartwright gets at the most ten thousand—five hundred a year."

His face showed so much quiet satisfaction, that I said, "Disgracefully little."

"What? Are you on the side of the Carthaginian?"

I recognised one of Uncle Terence's classical jokes.

"Not specially, but I think it only fair that one should pay for one's pleasures. There's no doubt that the man Cartwright as you call him, was a great pleasure to Aunt Catherine, for about eighteen months after her marriage, and before the marriage, too."

"Look here——"

He turned on me in the bullying way which I knew so well. But it was no time to quarrel.

"Let's agree sensibly to differ," I said, "on this point. What about the legacies? Did Dace get anything?"

"Four hundred. Buxey a thousand. I must say I'm surprised you take this line about Cartwright's share. Aunt Catherine evidently thought she was being too generous, because it was only Friday that she wrote to Smoult asking him to prepare a new will, in which Cartwright was to have nothing at all."

"A fourth will?"

"It was never executed or engrossed, of course—not even drafted. It was to be very like the old one, except that Cartwright got nothing and some of the legacies were changed. Dace, for example, got a big increase in his. A codicil would have done it, I should think, but apparently Aunt Catherine distrusted codicils—thought they always led to litigation. She was going to call and sign the new will some time next week. Of course, her instructions are quite inoperative. Her will, from the legal point of view, is the one she made in April."

We had been walking backwards and forwards on the lawn. At that moment we were opposite to the drawing-room window, and saw my uncle standing by it, watching us. There was nothing for it but to go up to him.

"I don't care to speak to that bounder," Bob muttered. "I suppose I must be civil for the time being."

"I hope you will," I said.

Bob and Uncle Hannibal shook hands.

"I've come round, more or less professionally," Bob said. "I don't know whether all my aunt's private papers and money are locked up. If not, they ought to be, until the time comes to go through them."

"Most of her private things were in the bureau in the boudoir. The police have the key of that and of the boudoir itself."

"Had she no other desk or private cupboard?"

"She used the desk in the drawing-room. I don't know about its being private. She kept one or two of the drawers locked."

"Are they still locked?"

"Yes."

"Where's the key?"

"I don't know. Probably in the bureau in the boudoir."

"Did you notice any stray keys in the bureau, Malcolm?"

"No. But I didn't look in the pigeon-holes at all."

"I should like to be sure that no unauthorised person can obtain access to those drawers."

"I should like to ask," my uncle said angrily, "why you're taking upon yourself to make these arrangements? I should have thought that job was either the police's or *yer* aunt's husband's."

"I am here, as a matter of fact, as an executor of my aunt's will. If you interfere, you may find yourself in an awkward position."

"Are you the only executor?"

"No. Malcolm's the other. But I am sure he'll understand if I say that he has no professional status."

"You're a pretty bloody conceited cad!"

Before I had time to do anything, they had come to blows, my cousin was sprawling on the grass, and my uncle walked back into the house. The housemaid's scared face appeared at the window of my aunt's bathroom.

"I should get up," I said. "It's silly to take this line.

He's naturally very much upset, and doesn't care to——"

Bob was on his feet by this time, and, after a glance at the drawing-room, turned towards the drive.

"I really think this is a matter to report to the police," he said. "I don't mind being knocked down—I daresay I asked for it—but I don't like having justice tampered with."

"How is he tampering with it?"

"By not letting me see that my aunt's effects are in safe keeping."

"He's done nothing to prevent you. We can go in now, if you like."

"I think I've done all I'm called upon to do."

"By the way, Bob. Here's something to show you I'm not entirely on Hannibal's side. Your mother has to see the police. Apparently she knew Aunt Catherine was going to buy the bottle. I told Hannibal she ought to see them. . . ."

"Is he trying to drag my mother in?"

"Not at all. I urged him to let them know they ought to see your mother. If he hasn't done so, you might take steps yourself."

"Thanks. I will. Father wired that he would arrive about four. I expect he'll come round here soon afterwards. I'm going to see the police now—about the inquest and so on. I expect it'll be on Tuesday. Meanwhile, keep your eyes open, my lad, and don't try playing any pranks. So long."

He went, and I was left with my thoughts once more. The news of the will did not excite me much. The time when we should all be enjoying our complex shares in my aunt's fortune seemed very remote. We had first to escape from the net of suspicions and alarms, reach the end of the nightmare. So far, each hour, instead of bringing any relief, had deepened the strain and added perplexities. There was no one on whom I could rely, or whom I could consult freely. I ought, I suppose, to have made common cause with Bob Carvel, but he was too antagonistic. His mother seemed too much in need of help herself to help me. Besides, she was surrounded by her family.

During luncheon, my uncle said suddenly, "If you'd like to look through *yer* aunt's things, Malcolm. I don't want to stop you. Go where you like and lock up what you like. I want everything to be regular."

"I wish you'd let Bob do it this morning. I don't really understand these things."

"I know. I'm sorry I lost my temper. Would you like to ring him up?"

"Oh, I should leave things as they are. I'll go through the drawers of the writing desk this afternoon. I don't see what else there is to be done. All Aunt Catherine's private things will be in her bedroom, I'm sure."

Dace brought in coffee, and suddenly my apprehension took a definite form, which was to harass me for the next twelve hours. All at once, I was afraid to drink—afraid of being poisoned. The fear was hardly rational, as I had seen my uncle pour out coffee, both for me and for himself, and drink from his own cup. Without sleight-of-hand, he could not have introduced anything into mine. However, I was so alarmed, that I left it untasted. I recalled vividly the scene of my aunt's death-struggle, pictured myself suddenly moaning, vomiting, and collapsing. My terror was, I felt, so obvious, that I went hurriedly into the drawing-room and ransacked the drawers. I found nothing in them of any importance.

(ii) *Afternoon*

The afternoon was terribly like the morning, except that my nerves were more on edge. For about an hour I played Handel and Bach, driving my uncle to the little smoking-room. At about three, Buxey brought me a telegram from my mother, which told me that my sister had had "a fine boy," and that all was well. I must have looked ill, for Buxey suggested my having a rest.

I went to my bedroom and lay down. There were no sounds from the boudoir, and it seemed incredible to me that only twenty-four hours before I had been eavesdropping with light-hearted enthusiasm—while twenty-four hours before that, I had been wandering idly through the mining market in the Stock Exchange. Now I seemed more likely to be a victim than an amateur detective, let alone a stockbroker. For half an hour or so I tried to go to sleep, but could not, and in the end decided to go into the garden.

On my way, I looked into the spare room in the front of the house. The carpet was rolled back, and one of the floor boards had been taken up. Superficially, my uncle's statement was confirmed. Once more I mooned about in the garden, went to the back of the house and ate a few peas— over about two-fifteenths of which I had a reversionary interest according to Bob—and then returned to the front garden. There I began climbing trees on the lawn. My fingers trembled, and I never dared go very high up. At length, when I had turned my attention to the trees on the south side of the house, my uncle put his head through the smoking-room window and shouted, "What on earth are you doing?"

My conduct may have been unbecoming, but I was surprised and pained at the reproof. My uncle also said something about giving me a lesson in using the mashie, if I wanted to do something strenuous, but I pretended not to hear and walked away. Another half-hour and it would be tea-time. I began to dread the meal, as I had dreaded drinking my coffee. Somehow the half-hour passed.

At tea, I saw my uncle looking at me with consternation, I was fingering my cup nervously, and not daring to drink, although I had poured out my own tea. Then a feeling of shame enabled me to master myself, for the moment. "If it must be, let it be," I thought, and took a big gulp. The taste was normal. A minute went by slowly, then another, then eight more. Nothing happened.

"Are you ill, Malcolm?" my uncle asked.

"Oh no. Only a bit—absent-minded."

For a quarter of an hour, I managed to make conversation with him. Then I saw Uncle Terence in the drive.

"Uncle Terence," I said, "at last."

"Go and meet him, Malcolm. I don't want to see him. I will, of course, if he insists. But if he doesn't, I don't see what good can come of it."

I went through the French window.

Uncle Terence shook hands with me very gravely indeed. "This is a lamentable business," he began. "I am only sorry I couldn't be here earlier, but it was ten last night when I found your aunt's telegram. I suppose Cartwright is in the house now?"

"Yes."

"I'll see him presently, perhaps. Meanwhile, if you don't mind, I wish to ask you several questions. Bob saw the police this morning—as representing the family, you know—and they were fairly open with him, I think. I shall visit the chief constable myself to-night. The people on the spot are pretty competent, and of course they don't want to call in Scotland Yard if they can help it. Still, I am a little disappointed there has been no development within the last twenty-four hours. To my mind, the case is a simple one."

Then, for some time, he proceeded to ask me a series of questions, his manner showing that he expected full and frank replies. I was not unmindful of the warning I had had from the police as to secrecy, or of my own resolve to be discreet, and my replies, though full, were not always very frank. I had leisure, as we walked, to observe his thin and refined face, beautiful, in spite of its holiday tan, as a cameo. He was tall, spare and graceful. I could not help contrasting the faded distinction of his appearance with the plebeian massiveness of Uncle Hannibal, and even while I was considering my answers, thought how Aunt Anne, with all her cultivation and her delicacy of instinct, had tired of her parchment husband, and longed for a more muscular embrace. What did her husband know or suspect? There were moments when I should have enjoyed startling his composure with my knowledge.

One thing he said which sounded almost as if he had read my thoughts, though I soon realised that he was not referring to his own affairs.

"I'm afraid, Malcolm, that there are many homes which appear superficially harmonious and united, where, if one looks deeply, one can discover all manner of vile complications. And in households where an imprudent and foolish marriage has been made—you know, I think what I mean—one may almost assume that the semblance of agreement is but a semblance, and that there are very dark patches below. I hate to say anything unfeeling about your poor aunt, but I have no doubt that she regretted her miserable marriage. She was preparing to revoke her will. I do not care to think how painful it must have been for her. She was not one of those to whom the admission of error comes easily. All we can do now is to avenge her death. It will give me the greatest satisfaction—mind, I am not speaking lightly or vindictively—to know that the guilty person has paid the penalty. I trust it will be as great a satisfaction to you."

"I dare say," I said, "we have different systems of moral philosophy. I agree with you completely in hoping that everything will soon be cleared up. If no one whom I know is involved, so much the better."

"I am afraid, Malcolm, you are blinding yourself to the facts."

"What are they? That's what I am continually asking myself."

"I used the word loosely, I concede. I was referring to motive, opportunity, and probability."

"By probability," I asked, thinking of my table, "do you mean murderous disposition?"

"In a sense, yes. It is quite clear to me, for example, that no member of your family or mine would commit a murder. This, of course, counts for nothing in a court of law, but when we look at the case rationally, unhampered by the rules of evidence—this coming from a barrister must sound heretical to you—we can come to certain conclusions at once, and we are justified in looking for facts to fit those conclusions."

He continued in this strain for some time, and I acquiesced with his sentiments, so that he should not think it necessary to be too careful with me. At length, he said, "For form's sake, I suppose I should see Cartwright."

"If you would rather not, I think he will understand. In fact, I know he will."

"Very well, then. As I said, I shall call on the chief constable this evening. I have one idea which I hope to follow up. I hardly expect it will yield any result, at this late stage, but no stone must be left unturned."

We parted at the gate where Robbins, still on duty, saluted reverently. Evidently Uncle Terence was in high favour with the police. "If it was he who committed the crime," I thought, "we shall have hard work to detect him." What trap was he setting? His suspicions at least pointed away from me and reinforced my own. Was it not foolish of me to have told him nothing of mine, to have confessed nothing of the terror I felt in having to stay on at Otho House? It was very foolish. Yet, suppose I was quite mistaken? Suppose by some extraordinary means, Uncle Terence had contrived to enter Otho House on Friday? Suppose he had a confederate in the house? Dace? I began to weave improbable plots —improbable, but possible. They involved, for the most part, the knowledge that Aunt Catherine intended to buy the bottle at Bales', and the substitution of another poisoned bottle for the one which she had bought. "Truth will out," I said to myself bitterly. "On the contrary, it won't."

(iii) *Evening*

At dinner, or rather the most ragged of cold suppers, all my fears returned with violence. I not only shrank from drinking, but also from eating. Instead of oxalic acid, I now began to dread other poisons, slower, perhaps, but no less horrible in effect. The terror persisted even when the meal was over and my uncle, as on the night before, had gone up to his room, leaving me alone downstairs. I pictured myself falling asleep and awakening suddenly in agonies. I reached such a frenzy that I almost rang up Dr. Bradford and asked him to give me all possible antidotes without delay. It was most unfair, I thought, that I should be deserted in Otho House. The police ought to have realised my danger. The Carvels ought to have insisted on my removal to their house. Yet I had only myself to blame. I had refused to associate myself with the Carvel interests, and had shown a rude resentment of their patronage.

I sat miserably in the drawing-room, and tried to read, after looking at the bookshelves. I seemed to remember stories in which clues had been obtained from libraries, through the absence or misplacing of a book. But the shelves gave me no hint of any kind. At about half-past nine, I thought I heard steps in the drive. As the curtains were not drawn and one light was burning, I did not care to go boldly to the window and look out. Instead, I moved idly to the door, hoping that if I was being watched I should give no sign of suspicion. Once in the hall, I ran to the dining-room and peered through a chink at the side of one of the curtains. I saw no one, and concluded that I had imagined the steps, when I heard the sound of a door shutting in the servants' quarters. There was perhaps nothing strange in this, as it was still early, and some of the servants would be about. I knew that Dace was supposed to go round the ground floor at ten, before retiring to his semi-basement. On going back to the drawing-room I drew the curtains, and again tried to read. Just as I was beginning to take a faint interest in my book, I heard more steps and, I thought, the sound of a low voice. I turned off the light, went to the window and saw three men walking on the grass beside the drive, their backs turned towards me. It was very dark, and I did not recognise any of them, though I took one for a policeman.

For the next half-hour, I imagined noises of all kinds. Every creak in the furniture or woodwork startled me. If the room had been invaded by masked figures holding pistols, I should not have been surprised. My thoughts began to lose their rational basis, and imported into the events of the last two days all manner of fantastic and uncanny details. I even went so far as to wonder whether I had murdered my aunt myself, under the influence of hypnotic suggestion, and whether I should not, in a second trance that night, betray my guilt to unknown watchers.

An hour passed, and still Dace did not come. Was he merely idle, or had he met with disaster? The maid-servants had a staircase of their own, and I should not in any case have heard them going to bed. I was tempted to seek companionship with Buxey. She had been exceedingly useful, and we owed such comfort as we had to her. Dace was either demoralised, or, conscious that he would have to find a new place, made no effort to attend to us.

"There is little doubt," I thought, "that I am in a house with a murderer." I had by now abandoned my fanciful idea of Maria Hall's share in the crime. Since my aunt's death, I had become a person of potential substance. Though the contents of her will were still a secret, they might well be known to an interested party. Not being a lawyer, I had only vague notions of how my share would devolve if I died intestate, and probably came near believing the principle of melodrama, that it would pass to the "nearest villain." There was thus a two-fold reason for an attempt on my life—my inheritance, and my knowledge, real or presumed, of the crime.

At length, after much distress, I made an effort to control myself. What was my knowledge of the crime? And what did I deduce from it? Once more I took refuge in pencil and paper, and, urging myself to shrink from no fact or no conclusion, sat down at the writing-table till midnight struck on the grandfather clock in the hall.

XIII

My Heroism

(Midnight, Sunday–Monday)

I HAVE already shown myself to be possessed of many odious qualities. I cannot, without distorting the facts of this story, conceal my greed, my indifference to the other people's feelings and my interest in my own, my timidity, idleness, and vacillation. I hope that I have not given the impression that my whole nature is summed up by these displeasing traits. But I know only too well, I have not so far been able to lay a fair claim to any admiration. Not one of my actions has been worthy of applause, not one of my thoughts has been illuminating in its grandeur. I write this not complacently, but to show that I might well be forgiven for exhibiting myself in a more favourable light and for describing, without false modesty, the few moments during which I become suddenly courageous. My hour of heroism is long overdue. But I give no guarantee that, when it comes, it will not properly belong to the cinema or the lunatic asylum.

When I went upstairs to my room, my nerves were still very much on edge, though I now suffered from an unnatural excitement rather than fear. I was both appalled and stimulated with what I had written. I laid my manuscript on my dressing-table, and read it, much as I had read Aunt Catherine's investment book, while undressing. When I had finished I put the MS. under my pillow, turned off the light, and got into bed. No light came through the keyhole of the door into my uncle's room, and for a while I heard no sound of any kind.

I do not think that at the moment of going to bed I had any definite plan. I had an idea that a crisis was not far off, but was more inclined to let it come of its own accord than

97

to bring it about deliberately. I soon found, however, that I could not possibly get any sleep, with my mind in such a turmoil. I remember feeling very hot, and trembling all over. It was then perhaps that my scheme, such as it was, began to form itself, though I am convinced that it was not fully developed till the moment that I put it into execution. While it took shape, and took possession of my thoughts as if dictated by another person, I heard a movement in my uncle's room, and saw the little point of light in the keyhole of the communicating door. Every minute I expected him to come into my room. But he did not, and the suspense in the end became so exhausting that I realised I must go, after one preparation, into his.

I got out of bed as noiselessly as I could, turned on the light, and found a blank sheet of paper. I spent another quarter of an hour writing, and then, taking my latest composition and what I had written in the drawing-room, I opened the communicating door.

When I saw my uncle sitting in his pyjamas on the side of his bed and staring at me in surprise, the last vestige of my normal prudence left me. I became an automaton, wound up, no doubt, by the tension of my own nerves, incapable of changing my purpose or adjusting myself to events as they befell.

As if of their own accord, my lips moved, and I found myself saying, "Look here, Uncle Hannibal. We can't go on like this any longer. We've got to have a talk and thrash things out. I've brought something with me that I'm going to read to you—two things, in fact—and I don't want you to——"

"I say, Malcolm, hadn't we better——"

"I don't want you to interrupt me in any way until I've read both of them. Sit there, as you are. I'll sit here."

I sat down opposite to him in a chair with its back to the window, and took the sheet I had last written. My uncle opened his mouth, but before he could speak I had begun to read.

"I, Malcolm Warren, hereby confess that I murdered my Aunt Catherine Cartwright.

"I have long had the hope that I should benefit financially by her death. Since living in London, I have found my expenses increase with my opportunities for spending. Though I am not at present heavily in debt, I have been eager for some time to live on a different scale. I thought also that I should be benefiting many people by my action—people who would make better use of my aunt's money than she can herself.

"For the last six weeks or so, I have been waiting for an invitation to visit Otho House. Such an invitation was overdue. Early in May, I obtained some oxalic acid crystals from a friend who had access to poisons. I will not disclose his name. I decided to bring the poison with me to Macebury in case I should have an opportunity of using it, but without any definite plan.

"On the evening of my arrival I was given a magnificent opportunity.

"I found the bottle containing Le Secret de Venus by the investment book when I went to the bureau. The bottle had already been opened. It was easy to take out the stopper, pour out a little of the preparation into an envelope (since destroyed) and substitute the poison. I had little difficulty the next morning in persuading my aunt to take a dose. The risk of being discovered was slight, as I could admit to handling the bottle and unlocking the bureau.

"My reason for confessing is that I have lost my nerve. I cannot stand the strain of the investigation any longer. Besides, I see that I may endanger innocent persons. I overrated my freedom from scruples of conscience.

                                        (Signed) "MALCOLM WARREN."

As soon as I had finished, I got up and put the confession on the bed beside my uncle. When I did so, he stood up, sweat pouring down his face, caught hold of my arm, and said, "For God's sake, Malcolm. . . ."

I slipped from his grasp, went back to my chair, and almost shouted at him, "Sit down, will you? I've got something else to read."

He sat down, and I began on the other manuscript.

CASE AGAINST HANNIBAL CARTWRIGHT

1. For many reasons, into which we need not enter, it was greatly to Cartwright's interest that his wife Catherine should die.

2. He had had some oxalic acid in his possession for some time, and decided to use it when he could safely do so.

3. His wife told him herself of her purchase of the tonic called "Le Secret de Venus," at Bales', last Friday morning.

4. He gathered that the bottle was in the bureau in her boudoir.

5. He knew that the contents of the bottle and oxalic acid crystals were not dissimilar.

6. His wife had been intending for some time to ask his nephew Malcolm Warren to come to the house for the week-end, and recently had shown eagerness that Warren should see her investment book.

7. Cartwright developed his plan by seeming to oppose his wife's intentions on these and other points.

8. He was informed that a rat had died under the boards of the spare room, and waited till this week-end approached before having the boards taken up. The result of this was that a visitor would have to sleep between his room and the boudoir.

9. His wife asked him to telegraph for Warren early last Friday. He sent the wire to Warren's home address, in order that he should not get it till the evening.

10. Cartwright persuaded his wife that she was too tired to wait up for Warren, and suggested that if she was eager for him to look at her investment book she might as well give him the key of the bureau in which it was. Cartwright mentioned that Warren might be summoned home to Somersetshire on Saturday, as his sister was having her first child.

11. Cartwright had beforehand oiled the hinges and lock of the door between his room and his nephew's, and also the hinges and lock of the door leading from the boudoir to the landing.

12. He expected that his nephew, after fetching the investment book, would leave the key on the dressing-table in his room.

13. He intended to obtain possession of the key when his nephew was asleep.

14. Warren made this unnecessary by going down into the hall for a few minutes after he had fetched the investment book. During this period it was easy for Cartwright to go into his nephew's room and take the key.

15. He waited till his nephew had fallen asleep, and went into the boudoir by the landing.

16. He found the bottle hidden by the blotter. When he had put the poison in, he left the bottle in a conspicuous position on the top of the blotter, so that it should not be overlooked, either by his wife, when she next went to the bureau, or by his nephew, who, he anticipated, would show some curiosity about it.

17. Careful as this part of Cartwright's plan was, he had entirely forgotten the possibility of leaving traces of his presence by finger-prints.

18. He restored the key to his nephew by going into his nephew's room early, on the pretext of discussing the time of his nephew's bath. Making as if to look out of the window, he dropped the key on to a handkerchief, so that it should make no sound. Warren distinctly remembers having covered the key with the handkerchief the night before.

19. Cartwright contrived to be away from Otho House on Saturday morning, so as to avoid being at hand during the administration of the poison and laying himself open to the charge of dealing negligently with the seizure. He counted on the fact that no one would be available with sufficient experience to give the correct antidote.

20.   He may have hoped that the death of Mrs. Cartwright would be ascribed to natural causes, as her heart was known to be unsound. Failing this, he assumed that suspicion would fall on his nephew.

21.   Later in the day, he realised his error in the matter of finger-prints. When Warren drew his attention to the wrapper of the bottle, and pointed to it lying in the fender of the drawing-room, Cartwright began to hope that he had left no finger-prints on the bottle itself, but only on the wrapper. He had an opportunity of destroying the wrapper both before and after he was questioned by the police, and in fact did destroy it.

22.   The above is supported by Warren's evidence as to

 (*a*) The change in the position of the bottle.

 (*b*) A light in Cartwright's room long after midnight, and a noise which awakened Warren.

 (*c*) Cartwright's manœuvre in restoring the key.

 (*d*) The presence of the wrapper in, and later its disappearance from, the drawing-room fender.

I read the document with its monotonous repetition of "Cartwright—Warren—Warren—Cartwright," mechanically, and without expression in my voice. At the end of each paragraph I gave my uncle a quick glance. He seemed every time I looked at him, to be growing larger and more powerful, the muscles in his legs and arms and chest swelling to a gigantic size. At the same time, I felt as if I were dwindling away, and had become a bird whose neck he could wring, an insect which he could crush with his foot, a tiny candle-flame which he could blow out. This sensation conformed with my purpose, and strengthened it. I was entirely at his mercy. He had by him my confession, which would explain my death, provided he killed me so that my death should resemble suicide. So far I had given no thought to the weapon he should use, and realised that I must myself provide him with one. Before I had finished reading I had made up my mind. His window was wide open at the bottom, and opened on to a minute stone balcony, such as is often seen in Victorian houses. As soon as I had done, I climbed over the window-sill, sat on the stone ledge of the balcony, and swung my feet over to the far side. Below me was a drop of twenty-five feet on to the steps at the end of the terrace.

My uncle, in his surprise, gave me time to complete my action. Then, when I saw his face and shoulders coming through the window, I said, so that there could be no mistake, "My confession will account for suicide."

He was so big that it was hard for him to climb out into the recess. I watched him dispassionately, and saw his arm stretching out towards my shoulder, as in slow motion. His hand touched me, and I fell—or seemed to fall.

XIV

Progress

(*Monday*, 1 A.M.)

THE events which I have just described are, as I now look
back on them, no more terrifying to me than memories of
many nightmares. They are indeed less painful to recall than
the agitation which tormented me almost all the Sunday.
Indeed, once I had gone into my uncle's bedroom, I felt no
more actual fear. I have often asked myself how it was
psychologically possible for me to act as I did. I do not care
to think that for an hour and a half I took leave of my senses.
In trying to rationalise my behaviour, I must conclude that
the strain of the previous thirty-six hours had been far more
intense than I realised. It may be that I have, in spite of
all my enlightened theories, a subconscious horror of murder
which dismayed me almost beyond endurance. I had become
nearly sure that my uncle was guilty, and thought I had
special knowledge of his guilt, unknown to anyone else. I
had been convinced that he intended to poison me. Why
then did I go out of my way to put myself so completely in
his power?

I am not a brave person. I am often bothered with fears
which have little foundation in fact, but, while a barking dog
in a street or a hissing swan on a river (I say it with shame)
will often give me acute discomfort, I never remember
fearing physical violence from a human being—and this
though I have no confidence in my powers of self-defence.
Why this should be so, I will not try to explain. It may be,
therefore, that in my desire to end my suspense I resolved
to persuade my uncle (if he was guilty) to use, instead of an
insidious means such as poison, which I dreaded, an open
violence towards me, of which I had no fear. I wrote "The

Case against Hannibal Cartwright", in the first instance, in order to force myself to face the facts. Later, when I had gone to bed, I resolved to confront my uncle with it suddenly, in order to determine from his reception of it whether he was guilty or not. It is harder to say why I wrote my spurious confession. (I say "spurious" so that none of my readers may suspect me of being the criminal. I am neither villain nor hero in this story.) Partly I wished to bring home to my uncle, in the event of his being no more guilty than I was, how we were both tarred with the same brush, and the greatness of our danger. But still more did I wish to take him by surprise—to bewilder him by first seeming to have no idea of his guilt and then confronting him with my intimate knowledge of his actions. Surely, under the strain of these odd psychological probings, he would reveal his secret? Later, as I was actually reading the indictment, my scheme grew still more desperate. Let him imagine that my confession would explain my death—let him, if he were guilty, attempt to murder me. Perhaps I relied, with the optimism of a lunatic, on my power to parry him, or call for help if he did attack me. But I think that by this time I had been goaded into complete recklessness. The thought that I might have to pass another day as wretched as Sunday was too horrible, and I wished at all costs to make a change in the situation. I climbed through the window because I wished to make the test conclusive— and at that point my desire for the truth became such a monomania that even the consideration of my own life weighed with me no longer.

Such may have been the sequence of my motives. But some will find it easier to believe that I was not quite responsible for my actions. I am tempted to agree with them.

I opened my eyes to find myself in my own bed, with my uncle patting my forehead with a wet towel.

"What happened?" I asked. "Am I hurt?"

"No, no. You came over a bit faint, that was all. Lie still, and I'll get you some brandy. There's some in my room."

He went and came back with a flask. I drank, and was filled with tranquillity.

"A fine scare you gave me," he continued, "coming into my room and reading out all that stuff—and then climbing out of the window like that. . . ."

"I wanted to see what you'd do."

"What did you think I'd do?"

"Well, you might have tried to push me over."

"Perhaps we'd better not talk about it just now."

Clearly he thought I was still light-headed.

"I want to talk about it," I said. "I'm quite all right now. I had to show you what your position is, and let you know what I know about Friday night, and so on. And then I thought that with my confession, if you were guilty, you might show it by trying to go for me."

"Seems to me a bit like putting pearls into vinegar to see if they're real. If they are, they melt. But about this confession of yours, Malcolm? That upset me rather. There's nothing in it, is there?"

"I swear there's no truth in it at all, and that I had nothing to do with Aunt Catherine's death."

"And I can swear the same to you—though by and by there'll be one or two things I can explain."

"First, we'd better burn what I wrote—both the things."

He put the papers in the empty grate, and lit them in several places.

"Didn't it strike you that, if I was guilty and wanted to get you out of the way, it would have been easy for me to shove you into your bedroom, phone up the police and give them your confession?"

"I could have said it wasn't true."

"But it would have been a bit awkward to explain away, wouldn't it?"

It would, I thought. When I had written it, it had appeared to me almost a master-stroke. Now I began to regard it as the work of a half-wit.

"It all goes to show," I said, "that I didn't really—from the emotional point of view, I mean—believe you guilty, though all the facts told me that you were. I couldn't seriously have thought you would attack me. When people hear a noise, they often go to look for burglars without taking any kind of weapon, simply to reassure themselves. They risk the hundred-to-one chance that a burglar may be there, and know that if they don't look they won't be able to go to sleep. It's fairly easy to face things that are coming at once and will be over in a few seconds. But instead of talking about this, we've got to settle other things. I think we might have everything out now. Why don't you sit down in that chair?"

He poured himself out a little brandy and sat down.

"I see," he said, "a good deal's got to come out, that I'd prefer not to have known."

"You needn't be afraid of me. Whether the police'll have to be told, we can decide later."

"Malcolm, do you still feel at all doubtful whether I did it or not?"

"I haven't the slightest doubt left. I know you didn't. Don't ask me to say how I know. I'm only puzzled by the evidence against you. It looks almost as if someone had forged it."

"I can explain a good deal of that away. I don't much like telling you the story, especially as you're poor Catherine's nephew. . . ."

"I suppose there's a woman in it?"

"There is."

"Then you needn't mind me. I have very liberal views on these matters—very different from the views Aunt Catherine would have taken."

He got up, went to the fireplace to see if my manuscripts were completely burnt, and sat down again. He told his story with such embarrassment, with so much hesitation and prompting from me, that I do not attempt to reproduce his actual words. He spent some time explaining to me, rather unnecessarily, why he had married Aunt Catherine, and what his early relations with her were. She had been infatuated with him. He admired her money and her "class", and in a general way thought she was a "very nice lady". Very soon after the marriage, he realised his folly. His wife was less generous than he had expected, and more tyrannical. She became jealous of him, and resented his being away from her. In fact, she treated him as if he were a "lady-companion". In course of time, she lost her infatuation, and, conscious that she had been humiliated and deceived by her marriage, she began almost to hate him. A more sensible woman would have acknowledged her mistake and pensioned off the unwanted husband. Catherine was too proud and vindictive to do this. She even went so far as to try to disguise her aversion from him, so that he should not leave her, and assured him from time to time that he might hope for a big legacy under her will. No doubt it was this that kept him at Otho House. Naturally this "keeping up of appearances" which she demanded and he acquiesced in was a great strain on both, and became more and more difficult. Indeed, it seemed inevitable that one of them should give up the struggle.

So far he had told me little that I had not guessed. Then he came to the woman—Jessie Toler, who was housemaid at Otho House from October 1927 to January 1928. She was "a stupid, pretty little thing". He had caught her one day crying because her mother was ill. She accepted his sympathy eagerly and gave him hers. The mother's illness became worse, and tender scenes more frequent. After all, it was "human companionship".

At this point I asked a very direct question.

"No," he said, "I didn't, though later we went pretty far."

My aunt dismissed Jessie in January 1928, giving inefficiency as the reason. She did not then, or at any time, directly accuse her husband of having been unfaithful to her. Unfortunately for him, he met Jessie one day in the lane near the Fernley golf links. She had found a situation in a house a mile away. He stopped and gave her a lift in his side-car. She was exceedingly "pathetic", complained of being overworked, and talked of her mother's illness, which had become very serious. He was "sorry for the poor little kid", and, of course, attracted. A fortnight later they met again, and she told him that her mother was dead. They met a third time early in May. It was her night out, and he motored her into Peterborough and gave her some supper. On the way back there was a romantic episode in a field. The fourth time they met, about the 20th May, her manner was different. She refused a lift and talked pointedly about the harm of not keeping to one's station in life. He was hurt at the change, and uneasy. He continued to go to the links by the same route, but never saw her again. This made him think that the meetings, except perhaps the first one, had not been accidents.

On the 1st of June he had an illiterate letter signed "Alf Toler, brother of the girl you've wronged", informing him that Jessie was going to have a baby. Convinced that he could not be the father, he took no notice. On the 7th another letter came, demanding a hundred and forty pounds "for nursing expenses and compensation", and suggesting that if there was no reply by return of post he would find himself in trouble. The address on the letter was a little tobacconist's in the village near the links. My uncle went to this address, intending to have it out with "Alf", but the old woman in charge would tell him nothing. He learnt at the golf club that Alf Toler had been a caddy there till he was dismissed for petty theft three years before. No one knew what had become of him since then. My uncle dared not make inquiries too openly, and did not care to write direct to Jessie. On the 11th, another letter arrived, threatening that if the money were not produced within a week a full account would be given to my aunt. The writer also mentioned my uncle's visit to the "poste restante", and said that he didn't intend to run the risk of being knocked down by such "a thumping great bully" by seeing him in person.

My uncle was by now thoroughly alarmed and distressed. It was clear that Jessie, of whom he had grown sentimentally fond, had been deceiving him. Either she had "got into trouble" (perhaps with one of the men-servants at the place where she worked), and was trying to put the blame on someone more responsible, or she was not going to have a child at all and had joined in Alf's scheme simply in order to extort money. In addition there was a sudden marked change in my aunt's behaviour towards him. She went about with an air of triumph, and took such small pains to conceal her contempt of him that he felt sure she must have some knowledge of his difficulties.

He kept the accusing letters in an attaché case in his bedroom. As he said, he had no writing-desk for his own use. On the morning of Thursday, June the 14th, the day before my arrival, he opened the case and found that the letters were missing. He had last seen them on the previous Tuesday, when he fastened them together with a rubber band. Their disappearance could only be explained by theft. Anyone could have obtained the key of the case while he was in the bathroom, and almost anyone could have forced the case open with a suitable key or even with no key at all; for the lock was simple and insecure. He at once suspected Dace, partly because Dace's manner towards him became suddenly more insolent, and partly because there was no one else to suspect. It was unlikely that my aunt would "do her own dirty work", however ready she was to have it done for her.

The loss of the letters disturbed him very greatly indeed. Not only did it make him think himself the victim of an elaborate plot, but he exaggerated the importance which the letters might have in the divorce court. He regarded them not merely as threats, but as actual evidence. Had he consulted a solicitor, his mind might have been made easier on this point. But he had no one to consult. He had all the horror felt by the ignorant for "the law", and was specially disinclined to go to a lawyer in Macebury. The firm of Dennis and Carvel had locally such prestige that he feared his secrets would be revealed to them despite professional etiquette.

He decided to go to a little man in London who had acted for him once or twice, but he was anxious to find the missing letters before he did so.

He was convinced that these letters were in my aunt's possession, and resolved to search her two most likely hiding-places, the bureau in the boudoir, and the locked drawers in the desk in the drawing-room. He knew that the key that fitted the latter, in common with other household keys, was kept in a small recess in the bureau. The key of the bureau my aunt kept with her permanently. To begin with he had no notion how he was to get possession of this key, and even thought of breaking open the bureau, so intent was he on carrying out his project. When, however, my aunt suggested asking me for the week-end, and mentioned that she wished for my advice as to her investments, he thought it might be possible to obtain access to the bureau through me. She was suddenly so eager for me to see her investment book that it was easy to persuade her (in part by seeming to oppose her) to let me have it after she had gone to bed. He hoped that she would give him the key outright, but when he found that it was to be passed on to me in an envelope he had to contrive to get it from me. As to this, my guesses in the "Case against Hannibal Cartwright" were fairly accurate, except that he had had no hand in the event which prevented me from sleeping in the spare room. Indeed he would have preferred that I should sleep there, so that there would have been less risk of my hearing him in the boudoir. My aunt was a very heavy sleeper, and he had little fear that he would awaken her. I was wrong in thinking him responsible for the scantiness of my bed-clothes, which was merely a piece of bad housekeeping, but right in supposing that he deliberately sent the telegram to my private address so as to delay my arrival at Macebury. There was, of course, the chance that my landlady would telephone the contents of the telegram to my office, but this he had to risk. Besides, he sent it as late as he dared. I was right also in my guess that Aunt Catherine had herself told him of her purchase of the bottle. "You can tell Anne," she had said on Saturday morning before our visit to the town, "that I got her that French pick-me-up at Bales' yesterday." Evidently she had not cared for him to know that she was taking it herself.

"You know the rest," he said. "I was waiting till you'd gone to sleep, but when you slipped downstairs you gave me a good opportunity. I got the key and nipped back to my room. I didn't dare to go to the boudoir till after two."

"Tell me exactly what happened then," I asked. "Did you wear gloves?"

"Of course not. I never thought the police would be dragged into it. When *yer* aunt found I'd taken back my own letters, she couldn't say anything, could she?"

"No. Did you find the letters?"

"The first thing I looked for was the keys of the drawing-room desk. I thought that, as you were allowed to rummage in the bureau, it wasn't likely that the letters would be lying about in a pigeon-hole. Anyhow, it was safer to search downstairs. I found the keys in a sort of ink-well—only there wasn't an ink-pot in it—underneath the blotter. I remember the bottle was there too, but I didn't pay much attention to it at the time. When I'd got the keys, I went down to the drawing-room and found the letters quite easily. They were in the second left-hand drawer of the desk. After that I put the keys back in the ink-well in the bureau, and shut the lid, without bothering much about the exact position of the bottle and blotter, etc. All I'd got to do then was to get the bureau key back to you. I managed that, as you guessed, when I came in to ask you about your bath. As to the bottle, Malcolm, I swear again that I never did any more than just move it out of the way. I never opened it, or tampered with it at all."

"And the wrapper?"

"I never thought about the wrapper."

"But I pointed it out to you in the drawing-room fender."

"If you did, I was so dazed, I didn't take it in. You see, I hadn't any idea that the wrapper was of any account at all."

"Then who took the wrapper?"

At this, my uncle was silent for a few minutes.

XV

The New Situation

(Monday, 1.30 A.M.)

I SEEM, during this visit to Otho House, several times to have been summing up the situation with an air of finality, only to find that before I had a chance of testing my theories a new set of facts confronted me. My thoughts were slower than events. On hearing my uncle's story, and being persuaded of his innocence, I should have liked at least a couple of hours with pencil and paper so as to remodel my ideas. I was, in spite of my attack of faintness, very wide awake, and fairly lucid in mind, and if left to myself might have made some progress. But my uncle was sitting miserably in my room, and I had to try to give him advice and comfort.

"You realise," I said, "the great thing we've got to decide is whether we're to tell your story to the police or not. These letters that you've been so bothered by aren't of much importance now. In any case, they weren't evidence against you, and even if they had been, there isn't any question of divorce any longer. Evidently you left finger-marks on the bureau, and the police know it. Presumably you didn't leave them on the bottle, or they'd have arrested you."

He winced, and I went on, "This must have puzzled them a lot at first. The fact that your finger-prints were found everywhere except on the bottle was a point in your favour, unless they took it for a very clever piece of bluff, and supposed that you deliberately didn't put gloves on till you touched the bottle. Their view must have altered when I told them about the wrapper. You almost certainly left finger-prints on the wrapper, and if they find it——"

"I'm done for, you mean?"

"No. But you'll have to tell your full story."

"Which they won't believe."

"They wouldn't, perhaps—but their judgment isn't final."

"Malcolm, is there any chance of my getting away?"

"Absolutely none. It would make things look far worse, if you tried. You'd certainly be caught, and there'd be much less likelihood of a jury accepting your version. I'm sure everything will come right in the end—after all, there are probably other clues the police know of and we don't—but in the meanwhile, we must both stay here and wait. Now, I don't want to frighten you, but if you are arrested I think it will be best for you to say nothing at all till you've seen a solicitor. I'll get hold of a good one for you. If the police question you, don't make any kind of statement or admission, and simply say that you reserve your defence. After all, there's nothing so very terrible in being arrested. Very often, I believe, they arrest the innocent so as to throw the criminal off his guard."

I let my uncle digest this crumb of comfort for a few minutes, and then asked, "How much do you suppose Dace knew of your relations with Jessie?"

"Well, I should have said, nothing at all."

"Mightn't he either have spied on you—or been told by the girl?"

"I was pretty careful. I don't think he could have seen anything. And Jessie didn't like him. He tried to—make up to her once, but she wasn't having any."

"Was that before or after you—became friendly with her?"

"Soon after, I think."

"Do you know if Dace knew Jessie's family—brother Alf, for instance?"

"I don't think so. Jessie didn't speak of him as if she had known of him before they met here."

"If it is Dace who stole your letters, we ought to be able to trace his finger-marks on them, and perhaps on your attaché-case too. Unless he's an ex-criminal, it's unlikely he'd have worn gloves. I think we'd better get a private detective to attend to that part of the business for us. I can't cope with finger-prints myself, can you?"

"No."

"Now the wrapper. I assume it wasn't accidentally destroyed. Who had an opportunity of taking it? Obviously I had, but I didn't. In fact I threw it into the fender myself. You had, but, unfortunately—or it may be fortunately—you didn't Who else? Any of the indoor staff? At first sight it looks as if the person who took the wrapper must have been the murderer. We can take it, I think, that anyone who left prints on the wrapper must have left prints on the bureau— except for people, such as the assistant at Bales', who may have touched the bottle before it came into Aunt Catherine's possession. If there are other people's prints besides ours on the bureau, we may be sure the police will be on the track. So that if the murderer took the wrapper, he will have destroyed it, unless——"

I stopped for a moment. I had been about to say, "unless the murderer is particularly brilliant and is able to remove his finger-prints and leave yours!" but I thought it better not to alarm my uncle with such a horrible possibility.

"Ten to one," I went on, "the murderer took the wrapper and destroyed it. Thus, as far as the police go, they will probably have at least three sets of prints on the bureau, and no wrapper to rule any of them out by negative evidence. This should leave you, me and the unknown equally suspect, except that I've accounted for my prints by a story which they must have found fairly credible, and you, so far from accounting for your prints told a few lies which they can disprove. But you had a pretty good reason for your lies, and when everything comes out they oughtn't to carry much weight."

"Should I make a clean breast of everything, right away?"

"I shouldn't, till you've seen a solicitor. There'll be plenty of time. Of course, we suspect Dace of having taken the wrapper, just as we suspect him of having stolen your letters. Do we suspect him of having murdered Aunt Catherine?"

"I should like to."

"So should I. But why should he do it?"

"Does he get a legacy, I wonder?"

"Yes. By the way, Uncle Hannibal, I'm going to break a vow and tell you that, according to Bob, you get about ten thousand pounds under the will. I wish it had been more. Don't say I told you."

"It's as much as I'd hoped for, if not more. I only hope— I'm spared to enjoy it."

"Of course you will be. But about Dace. He may have done the murder for his legacy, but I happen to know that if Aunt Catherine had lived, she would have made a new will, giving him a much bigger legacy. . . ."

"And me much less?"

"Yes."

"That looks bad."

"Perhaps, but it only underlines the motive that I'm afraid applies to all of us—Aunt Catherine's money. If Dace knew about the increased legacy, he obviously wouldn't have killed Aunt Catherine when he did. Of course, it may be one of life's little ironies that he should have chosen such a stupid moment. On the other hand, if he stole your letters, he was obviously in league with my aunt against you. She probably told him about the legacy, or may have paid him handsomely in cash. In any case, I can't see why he should murder her. But I'm inclined to suspect him of taking the wrapper. Yet why should he want it, if he was innocent? By taking it, he probably put his own finger-prints on it, which would be awkward for him if the police got hold of it. Is it possible that he had been tampering with the bureau and had tried to steal something from it? I wish it weren't so easy to invent reasons for actions—especially as one knows that the real reason is usually the one which seems least plausible."

My uncle stretched himself and got up.

"Well, Malcolm, you must be dead tired now. It isn't fair to keep you awake any longer. I'm frightfully grateful to you

116

for trying to help me—and for believing in me. Do you feel quite all right now?"

"Quite, thanks. We'll continue our talk after breakfast. Good-night."

"Good-night, old chap."

He turned out the light and went into his own room.

Before I fell asleep I had time to ask myself why I was so convinced of my uncle's innocence. The only reasons which I could find were:

(1) If he had put poison in the bottle, he would have had the sense to wear gloves.

(2) If he had been guilty, he could not have come so well out of my "test"—which, however foolishly conceived, was as it turned out, searching.

XVI

Monday Morning

I AWOKE to find that it was a quarter to eleven. No one had
called me. My clothes were lying disordered on a chair.
The wash-basin showed the remains of soapy water. I rang
the bell. It was answered, after about ten minutes, by Buxey.
She seemed startled, defiant, and yet sympathetic.

"Mr. Cartwright's gone, sir," she said.

"Gone? What do you mean?"

"The Inspector called about ten o'clock, and they went
away together. There's a note for you downstairs. I'll bring
it up, if you like."

"I wish you would. But how do you mean, Mr. Cartwright
went away with the Inspector? Was he——? Did he take
any luggage?"

"Yes, sir. They went to Mr. Cartwright's room and came
down with a suitcase, and went off in the Inspector's car."

"I see."

"Would you like some breakfast up here, sir?"

"Just a cup of tea and a little bread and butter. I'm afraid
it's very late. Was I called earlier?"

"No, sir. Dace went in the night, sir. When we came
down we couldn't find him, and his bedroom door was open,
He's taken all his things. I told Mr. Cartwright and asked if
I should call you, but he said let you sleep on as long as you
wanted."

"I see. Well, I'll have my bath now, and perhaps you'll
bring up the letter with my breakfast, will you?"

"Yes, I will."

Once more events had outstripped my thoughts. After my
bath, I found a tray of breakfast on my bed, and an envelope

addressed to "Mr. Malcolm Warren." I opened the letter, and read:

"Dear Sir,
    "I shall be most obliged if you will kindly call at the Police Station this morning, at your convenience.
                                "Your obedient servant,
                                        "AMOS GLAIZE,
                                            Police Inspector."

The letter was hurriedly written on a piece of Otho House notepaper.

I ate and dressed, and before going downstairs tried the door of my uncle's room; for it was my intention to take his attaché-case, which, as we believed, bore Dace's fingerprints, and Alf Toler's letters, if I could find them, into my custody. The communicating door, however, was locked, as also was the door in the passage. No doubt the police intended to search the room, though whether they still hoped to find the wrapper or some other piece of evidence I did not know. As I reached the head of the stairs, I saw through the landing window a motor stopping at the front door. I concluded that it must be the police arriving to resume their investigations, but when I had gone to the drawing-room Buxey brought me the cards of two newspaper reporters, and said that some gentlemen were very anxious to see me. I had not considered this form of molestation before, and asked her to tell them that I would see no one. I also urged her to be very careful what she said to them and to try to influence the other servants. I was eager to reach the police station as soon as possible, but felt compelled to wait until the intruders had gone. It was about five minutes before I heard the front door shut, and then a little group, as I could see from the north window, instead of going away in their motor, went round towards the back door. Though I was annoyed at their impertinence, I had no real authority to prevent them from talking to the servants at the back, and made a furtive escape by the front door.

Almost as soon as I had reached the main road, I was lucky enough to catch a bus, which took me to the middle of the town in a few minutes. I went straight to the police station and asked to see the Inspector. After a short delay, I was admitted to his presence. He greeted me with heavy civility.

"Good morning, Mr. Warren. I hope I haven't put you out by asking you to come here, but I was told you'd rather a bad night and thought you'd rather sleep on than have me disturb you."

"That's all right," I said. "I suppose, Mr. Cartwright——"

"I much regret to inform you, sir, that Mr. Cartwright is now under arrest. I'm sorry I couldn't prepare you for the shock, but, after all, it isn't as if Mr. Cartwright is any blood relation of yours, is it, and I don't suppose, except for your wish that justice should be done, you feel very strongly about it one way or the other."

He watched me carefully as he said this. I blushed and murmured something about "of course wishing for justice to be done," and he went on, "What I wanted to tell you, Mr. Warren, was that you are at liberty to go where you please, provided you let me have your address, and don't go more than three miles from the town. No doubt you will not care to stay at Otho House alone. . . ."

"No. I think I shall take a room at the Golden Crane. How long do you think it will be before I can go back to London?"

"I think we shall not require you here after the inquest, which is at two o'clock tomorrow afternoon. Of course you will have to attend the inquest. You'll get a formal notice to-night."

"I see."

"I can take it then, sir, that your address for to-night will be the Golden Crane?"

"Yes."

"Well, in that case, sir——"

He was clearly about to dismiss me.

"Can I see Mr. Cartwright?" I asked.

"Er, yes. I think we can arrange that, provided he wishes to see you. If you call here about six o'clock, I'll see what can be done."

"Thank you, I will. By the way, Inspector, can I take it that I am no longer under suspicion?"

He seemed to dislike my question, and paused a moment before answering.

"Isn't that rather like asking me when I stopped beating my wife? You must remember, Mr. Warren, we look at this case from the side of facts, not persons. The first facts we struck naturally involved you, as being the only person present when the deceased took the fatal dose. We don't, as I dare say you might be inclined to do, make a list of people who could have done it and tick 'em off one by one. I may say that at present the facts don't point to you at all. Of course, we're always on the look-out for new facts—we're never above owning up to a mistake—and I can't say where they mayn't lead. But at present you can consider yourself pretty well outside the picture, and I don't see any reason why you should be dragged into it again."

He took a step forward and held out his hand.

"And Dace," I said, retreating a pace so as to get my sentence in before shaking hands. "Have you arrested him?"

"Him?"

"You know he left Otho House early this morning?"

Again he looked resentful of my questioning, and again he replied more agreeably than his look led me to expect.

"Well, Mr. Warren. I don't want to make any needless mysteries. Dace asked our permission to quit the house, and we gave it him. . . ."

"When?" I asked. "This morning?"

The Inspector disregarded my question, which I had no courage to repeat, and continued, "We know exactly where he is, and are satisfied that we can find him whenever we wish to. You will see him, I dare say, at the inquest to-morrow. Now, Mr. Warren, I'm afraid I'm somewhat pressed for time this morning, and——"

We shook hands, and I said, "At six, then. Good-bye."

I had barely gone thirty yards from the police station when a little yellow-faced man accosted me with an ingratiating smile.

"Excuse me, sir," he said, "but are you Mr. Malcolm Warren?"

"Yes?"

"Well, sir, I wonder if you'd be so good as to give me a few particulars of——"

"Who are you?"

"I represent the Press, sir."

"What paper?"

He told me.

"I shall give you no particulars," I said, "and make no kind of statement. If I find your paper publishing any kind of story as coming from me, I shall immediately write to your rival the *Daily Blank*, and tell them that you've told a pack of lies."

"You might at any rate keep a civil tongue in your head," he answered. "I'm only doing my job, and there's no call for you to take up this high-and-mighty line. . . ."

I disengaged myself from him with some difficulty, but not before a colleague of his, posted at a strategic position, had taken a snapshot of me, which appeared the next day in the paper, and showed me with my hat on one side, chin raised absurdly in the air, and my left arm stretched out disdainfully.

After this, I went, by a circuitous route, to the Post Office where I sent off the following telegram to Lionel Edge, a friend of mine who was "making his way" at the criminal bar:

"Urgently want general and legal advice Cartwright case. Could you send trustworthy private investigator and/or

122

solicitor immediately. Staying night, Golden Crane, Mace-bury. Will wire any change address. Malcolm Warren."

I found a taxi as I came out of the Post Office, drove to the Golden Crane first, where I engaged a room, and then went on to Otho House. By the time I arrived, it was twenty minutes to one. I rang for Buxey at once. "I shall be spending the night at the Golden Crane," I said. "I don't know what you and the others are going to do, Buxey. I think you'd better ask Mr. Carvel for his advice."

"Mr. Carvel did call this morning, sir. He said we were free to do as we wished, subject, of course, to letting the police know where we were. He said he thought you'd be moving to his house to-night."

"Oh. Well, I don't think—I ought to trouble them."

"I said that, speaking for myself and Mrs. Dury, we didn't want to leave anyone in the lurch like, sir, and as a matter of fact, it would be a convenience if we could stay on here for a day or two, seeing as we both come from a distance. Angelica the kitchen-maid, went home this morning, and Ada's packing now."

I felt relieved that the matter had been taken out of my hands. My reading of detective stories had given me a few hints as to the handling of servants in a house of crime.

"Have the reporters gone, Buxey?"

"Oh, yes," she said contemptuously. "They motored Angelica to her home. A lot of nonsense she'll talk."

"And have the police been this morning?"

"There's two gentlemen of the police here now, sir."

"Oh, where are they?"

"They went up to Mr. Cartwright's bedroom. I don't know if they're still there. You will be taking lunch, sir, won't you?"

Doubts as to my legal rights to do so suddenly assailed me.

"I don't know if I ought to, as——"

"Surely, sir, there can't be any harm in that. And it's no trouble. You had so little for breakfast, too."

How easy it is, I thought, to manage servants if one lets them be motherly.

"Very well, Buxey. I should like something. Perhaps a couple of poached eggs."

"Oh, we can do better than that, sir."

I stopped her as she was going to the door.

"You don't happen to know Dace's address, do you? He comes from these parts, I believe?"

"Yes, sir. I don't know if his family lives near now—I don't think they do—but he's got a brother a footman at a big house Fernley way."

"Not the house that Jessie Toler went to, by any chance?"

"I can't say that for certain, sir. Jessie Toler went to Lady Blagrove's. That would be near Fernley, wouldn't it? Diswinter House, Paston, we used to re-address her letters to. I never kept up with her myself, nor Mrs. Dury either. She was not, if you'll excuse me, a very desirable young woman to my idea."

"Was she friendly with Dace?"

"At times they seemed to hit it off, though, on the whole, not as well as I'd have thought."

"Well, Buxey, if Dace sends you an address or lets you know where he is, you might tell me, will you?"

"Yes, I will, sir. And now I'll see about your lunch."

She went out, and I was left wondering what I ought to do about the attaché-case in my uncle's bedroom. I was greatly afraid that the searchers might, with their coarse thumbs obliterate the marks which we supposed Dace had left. It is true that Dace's conduct in this respect was not relevant to his complicity in the murder, yet I felt that the more strongly my uncle's story was corroborated, the more chance was there that he would be given the benefit of the doubt. Ought I to warn the police of these supposed finger-prints? If I did, I would almost certainly be asked awkward questions at the inquest, and might have to disclose part of my uncle's case while it was still very incomplete. I was indeed, in urgent need of advice. I decided that, on the whole, it was wiser to say nothing. If the police unwittingly destroyed one of our clues, they could be made to smart for it at the trial, and their bungling might tell in our favour. I much regretted that I had made no plan with my uncle in the event of his sudden arrest. Beyond urging him to say nothing precipitately, I had given him no advice. He had told the police that I had had a bad night. No doubt he did not wish to be confronted with me when he was taken away. Perhaps, poor man, he did not know how far he could trust me—or it may have been a streak of delicacy in the rough diamond.

Once more I sat and pondered, till Buxey sounded the gong.

XVII

My Mother's Letter

(Monday Afternoon)

I HAD come with just enough money for the week-end. No doubt it had crossed my mind that I might go away with more than I had brought. This hope, as far as it related to ready cash, was not to be fulfilled, and I had met with unforeseen expenses—nail-brush, telegrams, taxis, and at least one night at the Golden Crane. I had exactly eight shillings left, and the return-half of a week-end ticket, which would not be valid. Clearly, I had to borrow, and with this object rang up Bob Carvel immediately after luncheon; for, little as I cared to be indebted to him, he was the most likely lender.

He answered the telephone himself.

"Hullo—yes, Malcolm. I say, the pater called on you this morning, but you'd gone into the town. You're going to dig with us to-night, aren't you?"

"It's very kind of you, but I've booked a room at the Golden Crane. I didn't want to bother you, especially as——"

"Oh, rot. We've got two spare rooms."

"Well, I've taken mine, thanks very much, and I think I'd better stick to it. I really rang up to ask if you'd cash me a cheque—or rather lend me some money, because I haven't got a cheque with me. Could you make it ten pounds?"

"Righto. When do you want it?"

"I should rather like it today, if it isn't too much trouble. Shall I call at your office some time this afternoon? If you'd leave it in an envelope for me, I could get it any time."

"Very well. We close at six, you know."

"I'll be round before then. It's very good of you."

"Oh, that's all right. I'm sorry you won't let us put you up."

"How's Aunt Anne?"

"She's gone to London."

"To stay?"

"No, only for the day. She'll be back for dinner."

"And Uncle Terence?"

"He's here. I told you he went round to Otho House this morning. We're going to make arrangements about the funeral this afternoon."

"When will that be?"

"Wednesday morning, I should think. The inquest isn't till to-morrow afternoon, you know. They've got another one fixed for the morning—a street accident, quite a small affair."

"Well, I may see you this afternoon—but don't bother to stay in for me. Good-bye."

"Cheerio."

Relieved that the conversation was over, I went back to the drawing-room, where I sat down at the piano and played a few short pieces somewhat "sacred" in character. Then I paused, and, still sitting on the piano stool, thought of money once more—but this time with reference to Uncle Hannibal's defence. The costs of it were likely to be very large. It was lucky I should have my legacy to draw upon. My mother, too, would probably be willing to advance me something, though she might disapprove of my readiness to spend on behalf of one whom the family regarded as an enemy. I am glad to say I did not once ask myself if I were not being rather foolish in wasting my substance over Uncle Hannibal. The strain which I had undergone, and my close association with the murder, had given me, only temporarily, it may be, more elevated ideas as to the value and uses of money than those with which I had come to Otho House. The visit had presented itself to me as one of business rather than pleasure. Indeed I have made it painfully clear that the emotions with which I arrived were far from those of dis-interested affection for my relatives. But I was now so obsessed with the murder and its consequences, that my feelings and impulses were changed. I could no longer look forward and survey the course of my life stretching into the distance. My vision was bound by the horizon of a few hours, and all my energies were directed to their needs.

At about three, I went to my bedroom and packed. As I did so, I looked idly round the insignificant room in which I had received such powerful impressions. I noticed the door leading into the boudoir, with its keyhole through which I had heard the Inspector's examination of my uncle and Dace, the dressing-table on to which my uncle had dropped the stolen key, the grate in which he had burnt my confession and my indictment of him, the door leading into his room, through which I walked with bold desperation the night before. I rejoiced at the thought of going away from the room and Otho House for ever, and yet, at the same time, my joy was tinged with that melancholy which we feel when we leave any material object which has been closely bound up with our emotions. What ages I seemed to have lived through since Friday night, and how my purposes had changed. I recalled the first evening and the mercenary pleasures of the investment book; the second evening, when I fancied myself as a detective; the third evening, with its nervous crisis. It seemed absurd that I could ever have imagined myself able to play the detective, so strongly did I feel that my one function was now to aid the defence. And yet, the defence would best be served by a discovery of the real criminal. I put my hand in my pocket and pulled out the crumpled sheet of paper on which I had written my "agenda",[1] and was academically interested in seeing how far I had followed it up. There was little on which I could compliment myself. (i) The bottle had been bought at Bales'. (ii) Aunt Catherine was not known to have had visitors be-tween luncheon on Friday and my visit to her room on

[1] See page 64.

Saturday. (iii) It would have been almost impossible for visitors to come in unobserved during that period. (iv) As for police evidence, I had found out very little, except that the bottle seemed to bear no finger-marks other than my aunt's, while the fate of the wrapper had assumed a sudden and mysterious importance. (v) By accident, I had unearthed a domestic scandal, and had certain lines (Alf Toler's letters, Jessie Toler, Dace) on which to pursue it—though, on my theory, it only bore on the murder indirectly. (vi) I had summarised all unusual and suspicious events in "The Case against Hannibal Cartwright". They had been interpreted for me by my uncle, to my satisfaction. Indeed the only end still "ragged" was Maria Hall's telephone call, which probably was not an "end" at all. I had to confess that I had made no headway.

I shut my suitcase, sat on the bed, and lit a cigarette. Was there anything which I still ought to do before I left the house? In a few moments I should be driving away in a taxi to the Golden Crane, and if I wished to make any further investigations should have to conceal or explain my return. I tried the doors of my uncle's room. They were still locked. No other action suggested itself to me. In the end, I carried my luggage mournfully downstairs and telephoned for a taxi with a sense of failure.

It was nearly four o'clock when the taxi arrived. Buxey did not come to the door to see me off, probably because she did not want me to give her a tip. Though she had not been at Otho House during my childhood, she seemed to regard me as a boy, and no doubt felt that it would be improper to take money from me. I was grateful to her for not coming, as I wished to hoard my eight shillings till I had made certain that Bob would refill my note-case. Half-way along the drive, I saw the postman, and rapped on the window for the driver to stop. There was one letter for me, from my mother. I opened it when we had started again, but the motor shook so much that I decided not to try to decipher the flamboyant writing till I was in a less jolting seat.

I left my luggage at the Golden Crane, telling the porter to take it up to my room, and walked to Dennis & Carvel's office, which was barely two hundred yards away. I was received by a clerk, who told me that Mr. Robert was not in, but had left an envelope for me. I had no wish to meet either of the brothers Dennis, and went straight back to my hotel, with the feeling of increased confidence which ready money always gives me. The bedroom which had been given me was small, and looked out over some stabling and a garage. Its equipment was scanty and failed to come up to my standard in several particulars—no ash-tray, no waste-paper basket, clumsy Venetian blinds, window impossible to open, wardrobe with no hooks or shelves, no chest of drawers, cracked wash-basin, no tooth-glass. I began to unpack, and then remembered my mother's letter. The first three pages contained news of my sister, who was flourishing. The fourth page began thus:

"I'm afraid I haven't had much time to think of you at Macebury, or even to be properly grieved about Aunt Catherine. It is, of course, a terrible shock and surprise. I felt she might outlive us all. You didn't mention the cause of death in your wire, but I suppose it was her heart. No doubt you will have telegraphed for Uncle Terence, who will do all that is necessary. Isobel is really going on so well that I *could* come over for the funeral, but I don't see that I need, with you there to represent our branch of the family. I hope you will try to be helpful to everyone and smooth over any little friction there may be. It is far better always to avoid any unpleasantness, even if it means not speaking one's mind, and not insisting too much on one's rights.

"Aunt Fanny will probably join you, though I think she will be rather foolish if she does. It would be nice if you'd ask her to dinner when you get back to London, if she's still there. She would appreciate it very much, and you needn't spend a great deal. She doesn't take wine. Her trips to London are really rather pathetic. I'm sure she thinks she's 'doing the season'. Even though she stays at Wesley's Hotel, it costs her more than she can afford. She's full of little attentions, poor thing, and last Thursday morning a mysterious parcel arrived from one of the big stores containing some stuff in a bottle labelled 'Le Secret de Venus'. Monica says one of her friends told her it was made of monkey glands. It sounds a disgusting idea. Fanny probably thought it was a new kind of bath salts, and the pretty bottle took her fancy. I shouldn't be at all surprised if she sent one to poor Catherine.

"I must stop these ramblings now, as it's nearly time for church. Give suitable messages from me to everyone.
"With love from
"MOTHER.
"P.S.—Will you be home next week-end?
"P.S. (2)—I can't help feeling just a little excited!"

XVIII

Up a Tree

(Monday Evening)

AFTER reading my mother's letter, I sat on my bed for ten minutes, while an impulse to rush to the police station swung backwards and forwards through my mind like a pendulum. When I did rush, however, it was to the post office, where I sent off a telegram:

> "Mrs. Oldmarsh, Summer Coombe, Somersetshire.
> "On no account use Fanny's present, but preserve carefully under key. Most important. Writing. Address here Golden Crane Hotel. MALCOLM."

It might be that any telegrams sent off by me would be passed on to the police. If so, it could not be helped. I had at all costs to warn my mother against taking the mixture, and could only hope that my wording was obscure enough to hide my meaning from the inquisitive. It is true that I had no reason to suppose that even if Aunt Fanny had sent a poisoned bottle to Aunt Catherine, she would also send poison to my mother. Aunt Fanny was a poor creature, of feeble wits, the last person whom one would suspect of deep schemes or homicidal mania, but I dared take no risks. Indeed, I was in such an agony of mind that, on reaching the hotel, I went back to the post office again and sent off a second telegram:

> "Mrs. Oldmarsh, Summer Coombe, Somersetshire.
> "Please wire if my first telegram received and instructions obeyed also if anyone has used Fanny's present. Most anxious. MALCOLM."

Once more in the hotel, I ordered tea, and while waiting for it scrawled on a piece of paper:

"Bot. arr. S. Coombe Thurs. morn.

Bot. arr. Otho Thurs. morn. or(?) Wed. night.

? No bot. sent Otho. Coincidence?

? Visitors Otho Wed. night till Fri. noon."

The clock in the lounge struck five. In an hour's time I was to see my uncle. What should I tell him? What would he tell me? Would there be a microphone in his cell? If not that, an eavesdropper? The moments went by slowly, while my agitation and my feeling of impotence increased.

At twenty minutes to six I was still sitting in the lounge, with an agricultural paper on my knee, when the porter brought me a telegram.

"Malcolm Warren, Golden Crane, Macebury.

"Colles solicitor excellent experienced reliable arrives Macebury 10.27 to-night if possible. Failing that first thing to-morrow. Will report you on arrival.
LIONEL EDGE."

I was very glad to get this message, and set out to visit my uncle more cheerfully. On the way I bought 200 Craven "A" which I knew he smoked, three Edgar Wallaces, and a pack of cards. On my way to the "cells" a policeman asked me what the parcels contained. I gave them to him to examine, and they met with his approval. "You see, sir," he said, "we have to be careful about what's introduced here."

I found my uncle sitting in a wicker chair in a small plain room, which I felt might have been a study in a theological college—not that I had any experience of such places. I had to brace myself up for the shock of meeting him, and almost before my guide had left us alone, I said gushingly, "Good evening. You see, I've brought you something to read, some cards and cigarettes."

My uncle got up and we shook hands. I noticed that he was trembling. He thanked me awkwardly, and I went on—

"Someone is coming down this evening to help us with your defence. I think we'll soon be able to straighten things out. I hope you're not worrying too much."

"It's damned good of you," he said, "to bother about me like this. I sometimes think——"

He looked nervously at the door.

"Yes?"

"I don't want to seem ungrateful, but I sometimes think you'd better let me play a lone hand. I don't want to drag you or anyone else into this mess."

"But it's you who've been dragged in," I said, realising that the interview was likely to be both difficult and painful. "I'm at the Golden Crane now," I continued with deliberate irrelevance. "I moved there this afternoon."

He looked at me, I thought, with relief.

"You won't be sorry to have done with Otho House, I dare say. But you weren't turned out, I hope?"

"Oh, no. I just thought I'd be better on my own. I'm not very clear who has a legal right to stay there just now—if anyone has. Your room was locked up."

"Yes—er, they locked it when I was——"

I went close up to him.

"I suppose it contains," I whispered, "all it did last night?"

"So far as I know," he said huskily. He was clearly nervous of these intimate conversations being overheard, and I took up my earlier position.

"I slept till eleven this morning. I wasn't called. Dace seems to have flitted before the other servants got down."

"It doesn't surprise me."

"Now tell me, is there anything at all I can do for you beyond the arrangements I've already made?"

"I don't think there's anything, thanks."

"There's nothing you want fetching from Otho House?"

"I've got enough to go on with here. Besides, my things are all locked up, aren't they?"

"Yes, but I suppose I could get permission to go into your room under escort."

"Maybe. But I'd rather you didn't trouble. I feel I don't want to see the place again, and I'm sure you don't either."

Again I was surprised by his eagerness for me not to re-visit the scene of the crime.

"By the way," I said casually, "have you heard anything from Maria Hall again?"

"Maria Hall? Why on earth should I?"

"I've been a little puzzled by her telephone call."

"When did she telephone?"

"The night I arrived, Friday. Don't you remember, just as we were going up to bed?"

"Oh yes. But that was nothing—only to ask how *yer* Aunt was."

"But why did she want to know?"

"Haven't an idea. She'd been to tea the day before, and perhaps she thought *yer* Aunt was a bit off colour. There's no accountin' for what these old women do."

I looked at him intently, and he blushed.

"Good-bye," I said, holding out my hand. "I'm not going to worry you any more. Everything that can be done will be done. Try and take things calmly. There'll be a change for the better soon."

He wished me good-night and I went out, finding a con-stable just behind the door. I was glad that I had said nothing of importance.

My adviser was to arrive about half-past ten, at the earl-iest. This left me four vacant hours, with only dinner to fill them, and the general standard of the Golden Crane did not encourage me to expect much from that meal. Meanwhile, I was overwhelmed with my great secret, which threw doubt on so many fixed ideas and played havoc with alibis. I yearned for the coming of my confidant—the superman who would gather up my little twigs of knowledge and suspicion, and build them together into a nest of complete proof.

The weather was still uncertain, now hot, now cold. For some moments I wandered round the town, looking at the shops and wondering whether they were open or closed; for when open, they had none of that bold display, and when closed, none of that rigid fastness, to which I had grown accustomed in London. It was almost the first time since my childhood (when I used to steal away from Otho House to go to the cinema) that I had been "on my own" in Macebury, and unaccompanied by relations. I was impressed by the indefiniteness of the place, its lack of character, or rather the medley of its different characters. At one corner of the street one could fancy oneself in a Southern cathedral town. A few yards farther on, and one would find a garage, a Moorish café, and a hall of automatic machines, while behind them rose the spire of a chapel and a factory chimney. I was amazed at the number of stray cats, dogs, and children, and in one alley, hens. Every other second motor-bicycles hooted past me. What a place to live in, to be a citizen of! My thoughts turned to my Aunt Catherine, queen of the district, living with her prisoner of a husband a mile and a half away. A sudden revulsion against her way of life and her dominion overcame me. I realised how I had always detested Otho House, its solidity, its restraint upon free action and free speech, the tyranny of its large and ugly rooms, its flat and uninteresting garden. It was unbelievable that its power was at last ended, that it would no longer direct my life from afar, or, like an evil magnet, draw me back towards itself.

Yet even at that moment, I found myself sauntering past the straggling houses that bordered the main north road. It was still not much after half-past six, and I could dine at my convenience, provided I did not outrage provincial habits by demanding food at an unduly late hour. I decided to have one more look at Otho House. Whether I felt that I had taken too abrupt a departure from it that afternoon, and wished to bid it a more ceremonious farewell, or whether I still hoped that it would reveal me yet another secret, I do not know. I think my uncle's evident relief that I had gone to the Golden Crane, and his unwillingness that I should revisit Otho House, had made my contrary mind regret that I had so decisively changed my quarters. At all events, it was a walk and would kill time. If an excuse were needed, I could say that I was intent on giving Buxey the tip which her loyalty had earned many times. As I passed the Carvels' house, I quickened my pace, and did not slacken it till I had reached my aunt's garden.

While I walked slowly up the drive and the square house came into view, I made the most of my hatred. "This," I thought, "is where I have spent so many tedious Sunday afternoons. This is the seat of empire from which we were all ruled. Never again. Never again." I saw the tennis-court on which, as a child, I was not allowed to play, though when my Uncle John Dennis played, I had to pick up the balls; the greenhouse in which I had broken two panes of glass; the potting-shed in which I hid at church-time. The memories of a thousand trivialities came over me. Never again. Soon, I hoped, very soon, the pompous house would fall beneath the auctioneer's hammer, would become the prey of new owners who would set little store by its traditions, violate all that had been most sacred, torture it into a new form. I almost wished that it might become an inebriates' home or a house of ill-fame, till suddenly I recovered my sense of proportion, and said to myself, "This is where your kind rich aunt allowed you to spend a good part of your holidays. Here she gave you food and lodging, and once, even, a new suit. Here she was murdered last Saturday morning, with you at her bedside. Deal gently with the past, and turn your thoughts to the present. Why have you come here again?"

I had come, I thought, answering myself, to have a last look round. Was there still anything, however trifling, which had happened since my first arrival, that I did not thoroughly understand, any event without apparent cause, any action without apparent motive? Maria Hall? Maria Hall? Why did she telephone? Did she telephone? The bell had rung and my uncle had spoken. "Going on fine, thanks, . . ." he had said, "had dinner in her boudoir. . . . Good-night." Why did Maria take this interest in my aunt, and what reason had I for thinking it was she who telephoned? My uncle's word. When he swore his innocence to me, I believed him. When, that morning, he had said he *remembered* Maria's telephone call, I could not believe him.

I was filled with a sudden excitement. Clearly he had a clue in which I did not share. Hurriedly I tried to think of all the conversations I had had with him since my coming. The confidences of the first night—nothing in them. His interest in my bath the next morning—that had been explained. His kindness in taking me into Macebury—natural goodness of heart. His grimness and remoteness after the murder. This was not only shock, or grief, or even personal apprehension, but there was some other feeling behind it which I had not fathomed. The wrapper? I had begun by thinking that my uncle had destroyed it. This he had denied in his midnight confession, and I still believed that he had told me nothing but the truth during those tense moments. Nothing but the truth—but not the whole truth, perhaps. The period when he had seemed to be avoiding me—Saturday evening and all Sunday till bedtime, was the one to examine most carefully. What had he done, or said, during that time?

I strode rapidly round the house in a big circle and tried to live those hours over again. My visit to Aunt Anne. A miserable meal. My uncle's flight to bed. My early rising, and a cold, hungry prowl round the gardens. Breakfast. The Sunday papers. My uncle's refuge in the garage. Bob Carvel's visit. Painful scene between him and my uncle. Luncheon and my first attack of nerves. My uncle's flight to the smoking-room. Another stroll in the garden, during which—

what memory was it that rankled? What had happened that hurt my feelings during that hour before tea?

Vaguely I looked round the garden, as if seeking a material clue. I was standing on the south side of the house, beside a clump of trees, one of which, an enormous birch with easily graded boughs, almost invited me to climb it. In a flash the episode for which I was searching came back to me, and I had a vivid picture of my two hands on the lowest bough, and of my uncle's head appearing at the same moment through the smoking-room window. Again, I seemed to hear him shout, half in anger, half in alarm, "What on earth are you doing?"

What on earth was I doing? I had been about to climb the big birch in front of the smoking-room window. Why the reprimand? Was it nervous exasperation at my ungraceful antics, or was there a deeper cause? With careful deliberation, I began to climb again.

In a hollow space formed by the union of the four principal boughs, I found a small red book, shabby and damp, with a sheet of notepaper roughly folded inside, and a thin cardboard box, such as is used for packing scent-bottles, containing something heavy. An unbroken label ran round it, bearing in fancy lettering the words, "Le Secret de Venus," while a circular slip gummed on one corner showed its origin—"D. & S. Bales, 29 High Street, Macebury."

Keeping an eye on the windows of the house, I climbed down with my discoveries. I did not dare to examine them further till I had crept into a thick shrubbery which hid me on every side.

The book was *The Student's Handbook of Forensic Medicine*, the sixth edition, dated 1895. On the fly-leaf, in faded ink, was the signature, "John Dennis, Macebury, September 1902." I was familiar with similar signatures in many of the older books in my aunt's library. The sheet of notepaper bore the big black heading which appeared like a threat at the beginning of all Aunt Catherine's letters, and the writing was hers.

"Telephone and Telegrams: OTHO HOUSE,
        Macebury 0597.   Near MACEBURY.
                                        Friday, June 15th, 1928.

"MY DEAR FANNY,

"Many thanks for your letter, and still more for your touching little present which arrived yesterday morning. You don't say whether you have tried the stuff yourself!! Probably not. I have been bolder and took a dose yesterday, without feeling any ill effects *so far.* Indeed, rather the contrary, for I am full of energy to-day and ready for anything. I shall try another dose to-morrow. I always think it is unwise to take a new tonic too *liberally* at first.

"I hope you are enjoying your visit to London, though I think it is rather foolish of you, at your age, to waste your health and your money in trying to have a 'season'. Your hotel does not sound very interesting; in fact, I am afraid I should find it rather *dull* after the Metropole, where I always used to stay with John. Still, no doubt, you require a change from Bude. By the way, you mustn't think that we are quite so countrified here as you are. As a matter of fact the preparation you sent me can be bought at Bales', our chemist's here. They have quite a display of the bottles in their window. I'm not sure I approve of exhibiting the stuff like this, as part of the *brochure* isn't at all respectable—in fact, is full of *unpleasant* suggestions. Perhaps you did not read it very carefully. I keep the bottle you sent me out of sight of the servants, and if you have bought one for yourself I advise you to do the same.

"I am hoping Malcolm will come to us to-night for the week-end. He's a change from the Carvels, even if a little spoilt. Hannibal is playing golf this afternoon. Terence's wretched son-in-law has been giving us more trouble. This time I have refused to—there's my tea coming in. I will continue later."

At this point the writing ceased, about four lines above the bottom of the page.

XIX

Catastrophe

(Monday, 7.17 p.m.)

MY right pocket bulged with *Forensic Medicine*, my left
pocket with the "Secret of Venus" in its cardboard case.
Aunt Catherine's letter to Aunt Fanny was in my notecase.
I dared not leave my three clues any longer in their hiding-
place. More than ever I longed for Colles' arrival, so that he
might share some of my responsibility. A wind was rising,
and howled through the trees of my aunt's garden, driving
a cluster of thundery clouds across the sky. Overwhelmed
with new knowledge, I was all eagerness to be gone, and
had no thoughts for Buxey's tip or ceremonial farewells. A
bird of ill-omen, I flew down the drive and into the main
road, my weighted coat flapping round me like little wings.
If there had been a taxi, I should have taken it, but there
was none.

As I passed the Carvels' house. I was stopped by the clear,
melodious voice of Uncle Terence.

"Why so fast, Malcolm? And whither away?"

"To the Golden Crane," I shouted breathlessly. "It's going ·
to rain."

He came towards the gate.

"Well, take shelter with us. And have some dinner. We're
none of us dressing, of course."

"Oh, thank you," I said, "but really, I——"

"Now, Malcolm," he said in his most urbane voice, "if
you won't come in, I shall think it really uncivil of you.
We're already rather hurt that you won't let us put you up
for the night, but I quite understand you may feel more
independent at your hotel. But I insist upon your dining
with us. Our fare is not very grand, but I can promise you

it's no worse than you would get at the Crane. Come in."

He opened the gate, and I went before him into the house. I remembered my mother's advice that I was to do my best to keep the peace, and resolved to follow it as far as I could.

"You're very good," I said. "I've just been to Otho House to fetch something I'd forgotten. Is Bob about?"

"I left him writing some letters. Muriel and Hetty are in their room. I think we might go into the smoking-room. When Bob comes, he'll mix you a cocktail. I don't take them myself. We dine at eight. Aunt Anne went to London this morning, but she should be back fairly punctually. Do you smoke a pipe?"

"No—I have some cigarettes, thanks."

"Well, Malcolm, I feel I stand rather *in loco parentis* to you, and you must excuse me if I try to give you some advice. Without in any way wishing to criticise your motives, I must say I think you've taken up a misguided attitude in this affair. Of course, you may have felt that we were all banded together against Cartwright, and it was, no doubt, a generous impulse which led you to associate yourself with him. I applaud you for it, but you must realise that this is really no time for quixotry. I may tell you, the case seems to me absolutely conclusive. There was one little piece of evidence wanting, but even that has now been—supplied. We are all, unfortunately, bound to figure fairly largely in the public eye, as a result of this case—and as a matter of common prudence, it is not very wise of you to cut adrift from what I may call the family, and ally yourself with the intruder, who is also the criminal. It shows a callous indifference, not only for us, but for your poor aunt. I venture to say, Malcolm, that when the sentence of death is pronounced, you will be seen in a very ugly light, if you persist in abetting the defence. As a stockbroker, you have to some extent a public position—that is to say, instead of being independent, like an artist or a writer, you belong to a corporate body which has, I should imagine, over some things a fairly rigid code. I do not think that, if things go as

I am convinced they will, your future in Throgmorton Street will be a very happy one."

He paused, and looked at me gravely, his delicately shaped head slightly on one side, his pale lips parted in a deprecating smile that was in no way allied to laughter.

"Don't think," I said, "I resent what you're saying. I believe I see your point. But I—er—happen to have certain ideas as to this case, which I know you do not share, and no right-minded person can blame me for acting up to them."

He nodded.

"Oh, I am well prepared to believe in the fineness of your sentiments. But tell me, Malcolm, exactly why are you convinced of Cartwright's innocence?"

I blushed.

"I think my reasons are best left to counsel for the defence."

"I'm not asking you to give away your case, of course. But perhaps you'll tell me this. Is your conviction based merely upon intuition, or upon any piece of evidence that would carry weight in a court of law?"

I said nothing, and my uncle tapped the arm of his chair impatiently.

"I take it," he went on, "that your silence implies both. I can't believe you so foolish as to rely upon intuition alone, and I can't believe that you can have any evidence strong enough to influence you without the help of your 'intuition'."

"May I ask you," I said, "why you believe Cartwright to be guilty?"

"You mustn't think for a moment that I am in the complete confidence of the police, but let me give you my idea of how to-morrow's inquest will go. First, you will be called and very fully examined as to your story. From some little hints that have been dropped, I gather that your evidence is by no means entirely favourable to Cartwright. However, let that pass. I don't want to suggest to you anything so ugly as perjury!"

He darted a quick glance at me, and continued:

"Next, I suppose, we shall have Dr. Bradford, who will reveal how he came so quickly to the conclusion that some poison had been administered. After him, I should think they will call Dr. Mathews so as to complete the medical evidence. He will deal with the result of the autopsy, and Bradford will get a few pats on the back for the speed and accuracy of his diagnosis. Then probably they will want evidence as to Catherine's state of mind, so as to exclude suicide. You will already have given some evidence as to this, and more will be supplied by Buxey, possibly Dace, and my wife, who will state that Catherine had the intention of buying the mixture at Bales' on Friday morning. Then the definitely police part of the proceedings will begin. The shop assistant from Bales' will testify to the purchase of the bottle on Friday. Inspector Glaize and the finger-print man will depose to having found Cartwright's prints on the bureau, inside the bureau, on the blotter, on the wrapper of the bottle—and on the bottle itself."

I started when I heard this, though it in no way contradicted Uncle Hannibal's story. But I had assumed that the bottle would not bear his finger-prints, and was prepared to explain the prints on the wrapper by suggesting that he had picked it up from the fender and dropped it again. Meanwhile, Uncle Terence was watching me, and his pale green eyes glowed with little flames of triumph.

"They may also call Smoult, Catherine's lawyer, to prove that he had instructions to alter her will, so as to supply motive. No doubt there are many corroborative details which I have not mentioned, but I think I have given you the essence of the case."

He leant back in his chair, joining the tips of his fingers and lowered his eyelids. Without raising them, he continued: "Now you see why I think you should adopt an attitude at least of impartiality."

"Are you," I said, "really eager for justice to be done?"

While he was still staring at me, with amazement at my

question, my cousin Bob came it. "Hello," he said, and the tension was relaxed.

"Malcolm is dining with us to-night, Bob. Would you tell Alice? And I'm sure he'd like a cocktail."

"Righto. What's your fancy, Malcolm?"

"Could I have a Gimlet?"

"Yes, rather, though there may not be any ice."

Bob went in and out of the room, making his preparations, and conversation grew spasmodic. Presently Muriel and Hetty came in, and I had to greet them with a show of warmth.

"When is Aunt Anne coming back?" I asked, forgetting that I had been told two or three times already.

"Her train was due in four minutes ago," said Muriel, "that is, if she caught the one she expected. But she said we were not to keep dinner waiting, as she might be meeting a friend and stay for the 8.17, and have dinner on the train."

"That's the train I caught on Friday," I said. "I didn't know there was a restaurant car, and had dinner beforehand."

"There's something to be said for living on a main line, isn't there?"

I agreed, and made a remark with which my cousins agreed in their turn. Indeed, we were all terribly careful to avoid any statement that might be controversial. Uncle Terence left us, to prepare for dinner. Bob showed me where I could wash my hands. I had been conscious of his sisters' eyes on my bulging pockets, which I did not care to empty in spite of the damage to my coat. No doubt my cousins thought it was part of my usual uncouthness to go about in such a fashion. Cocktails, another cigarette and more talk. Ten minutes past eight. "Dinner is served, sir." "Shall we go in, Dad?" "Very well."

The food and wine were good. I remembered my mother saying once, "Terence could never save. Even when he was making five thousand a year at the bar, he always spent up to the hilt."

The women left the dining-room, and Uncle Terence offered me a cigar. Every moment I felt my position as a guest growing more and more irksome. Nine o'clock.

"A little more port, Malcolm? Or would you like some brandy?"

"No, thank you."

"You young men are very abstemious nowadays. Bob hardly touches alcohol. In my young days——"

A motor stopped at the gate, and my uncle, who sat facing the window, got up suddenly.

"Glaize, by Jove."

A moment later Alice came in.

"Please, sir, would you see Inspector Glaize?"

"All right, Alice. Show him into the morning-room, will you? Excuse me, Malcolm. This may be interesting."

He went out, and I sat looking at Bob, who was on the other side of the table. A minute passed and we did not speak, then another. I fiddled nervously with a square of morocco leather tooled in gilt, which had acted as doily to my finger-bowl.

"Rather nice, isn't it?" said Bob. "Mother did a whole set of them. You haven't seen her bookbindings, have you?"

Without answering, I continued to stare at him, and something horrible must have crept into my expression, for he suddenly grew pale, and his hand trembled.

"What is the matter?" he asked. "Why don't you speak?"

I cannot have been more than a minute before I did speak, but in that minute, despite the hideous suspicion which had at last become a certainty, I had the memory of a thousand little humiliations which I had suffered at his hands, the many times when, in comparison with him, I had been made to seem awkward, inferior or ridiculous. Now, for one instant, I had the whip-hand over him, and knew that with one sentence I could so drive home my momentary advantage that in our future meetings it would be he who would feel discomfort, he who would shrink away with mumbled excuses, and flee if ever I chose to pursue. Wide-eyed, as in a trance, I fought with the cruel impulse, and in the end my softer nature won.

I lowered my gaze and said, "Prepare yourself for something very awful. Have some brandy."

I rose to get the bottle, but as soon as I was on my feet the door opened, and Uncle Terence, his ivory cheeks now ashen, his lips shaking, and his eyes filled with dismay, tottered into the room, and, still clutching the door-handle, beckoned desperately to his son. Bob, with a look of terror on his face that I should not have imagined possible, hurried to the door, and father and son went out together, leaving me alone.

The sentence which I had in mind to utter, but did not, was suggested to me by a few lines on page 257 of *Forensic Medicine*, which I had read in the garden at Otho House—

"Does your mother use much oxalic acid for her leather-work?"

XX

Appendix A

The Story of Anne Carvel

(Based upon information from the police, Hannibal Cartwright and Colles, and my own reconstruction of the facts)

FEW echoes of the scandal which sent Sir James Teirson to a French gaol for six months, and disgraced Augusta Teirson in the eyes of a little clique of Riviera residents, reached England. Indeed, beyond the fact that Teirson had committed some kind of fraud, I have no idea what his offence was. Three hundred thousand francs could have saved him, if the money had arrived by Wednesday, June 20, but it did not arrive. Terence had never cared for his daughter Augusta, and disapproved of her marriage and of her living out of England. He had always been convinced that her husband was a ne'er-do-well, and had more than once said that the best thing was to give him rope to hang himself. Augusta had no one to whom she could turn except her mother. On June 9, Anne received a telegram begging for help, and on the 12th a desperate letter. She at once telegraphed and wrote to her husband, who replied by telegraphing, "Let James stew in own juice. Neither can nor wish to help." She then approached Aunt Catherine. Three hundred thousand francs—two thousand five hundred pounds—about an eighth of what my aunt (as we, her executors, found) had on deposit at the bank. Aunt Catherine made comments, offered advice, but would not give or lend a single penny. She had never liked Augusta.

Here lay the motive on which Anne laid stress in her confession to the police, but there was another and stronger motive which she did not care to make public.

When my Aunt Catherine had married Hannibal, Anne had taken neither side. She was polite to the intruder, but did not seek his company. He, for his part, was frightened of her, and never quite lost his fear. In the early spring of 1928, chance caused them to meet more frequently than before. Whether it was the season of the year, the attraction of opposites, some pathological change in Anne, the conduct of her husband, or simply a nervous desire for novelty, she fell in love with him. For a while she concealed her passion—indeed, she strove always to conceal it, not wishing to embarrass him. Gradually their friendship became more intimate, till he had no secrets which she did not share. She even learnt of his trouble with Jessie Toler, and instead of being indignant or disgusted, found herself even more strongly drawn towards him.

At the same time as her love for Hannibal increased, so did her acquaintance with Aunt Catherine. When the boudoir and adjoining bedroom were being redecorated, she had formed the habit of visiting Otho House every day, and continued to do so after the work was finished. No doubt such visits gave her a pretext for seeing Hannibal. So it was that Aunt Catherine, who suspected nothing of Anne's secret, disclosed her plans for the alteration of her will and the divorce which should fling Hannibal into an ignominious poverty. Even with Anne, Catherine was guarded as to the grounds of the divorce and the source of her knowledge, but Anne had heard the other side of the story. The murder of Aunt Catherine would thus not only secure the future of the miserable Augusta, but it would leave Hannibal rich for life and free. I think it is probable that Anne did not know how far the bequests to Hannibal had already been reduced.

About the beginning of May, Anne thought she had discovered in herself the symptoms of an incurable disease. She was liable from time to time to feel acute anxiety over her health. In the past, these attacks of nerves had subsided gradually, leaving a period of calm before the next onset. This time her emotions were so highly wrought that the attack was almost mania. In spite of herself, she gave some suggestion of her fear to Hannibal. To the rest of her family she admitted only that she was "run down", as indeed she was. For some weeks she would consult no doctor, imagining that when she did so he would plunge her straightway into the preparation for a horrible death. Why should she not live while she could, and see and help her beloved? In the end she was persuaded by Hannibal to see a specialist in London.

Harassed by these three troubles—her own health, and her daughter's and Hannibal's plights—she visited Aunt Catherine on Thursday, June the 14th. Maria Hall was paying one of her rare calls. Aunt Catherine was having tea in bed, while the two women had theirs at a little table near the window. Mrs. Hall left at about half-past five, and Anne once more mentioned Augusta and her need for money. Aunt Catherine still refused to help. "I am tired," she said, "of being pestered by beggars." Perhaps in the hope of gaining pity, Anne referred to her visit to the specialist which she had planned for the next day. Again Aunt Catherine showed little sympathy. She didn't "believe in doctors". Look how they had treated her when she had trouble with her skin. What Anne wanted was a tonic—"You'll see some stuff Fanny sent me in the bureau over there. I took a dose before you came, and think it's done me good already."

Obediently Anne went to the open bureau and looked at the bottle, though she did not touch it. "But you can get this at Bales'," she said.

"Can you? How like Fanny to think she's got hold of something new! But it does seem to be a remarkable mixture. I'll get you a bottle to-morrow when I drive into the town."

Anne thanked her, and referred once more to Augusta.

"I shall be obliged if you will not mention the woman's name again. If she's married a crook of a husband—and we all warned her—let her take the consequences." And so on, till Anne left.

That night Anne was sleepless. The thought of her visit

to the doctor—the beginning of the end—terrified her, while her inability to help her daughter or Hannibal filled her with desperate anger. Was there no way out, no way of "ridding the world of a silly and selfish old woman?" (The last phrase comes from Anne's confession.) Thus the scheme came into being.

The next morning, before catching her train, Anne went to Otho House. In an envelope in her bag was an ounce of oxalic acid—which she had long used for her leatherwork. Her last supply had not been obtained locally. As usual she was shown upstairs into the gorgeous bedroom. My aunt was still in bed, gay, resolute, and cruel. Again Anne mentioned Augusta—a last chance for Aunt Catherine to save her, and herself. Aunt Catherine spurned the chance. "Why don't you think of yourself, Anne, instead of fussing about this wretched girl of yours? You can't help her, and I won't. As for you, what you want is a good tonic, as I told you yesterday. Let me give you a dose of Fanny's mixture. You can take it here if you like."

"It's very kind of you, I think it's rather soon after breakfast. If I could take a little with me, I could drink it in the train. I have an empty envelope with me."

"All right., The bureau's locked, though. Here's the key."

Anne took the key in her gloved fingers, went behind the screen into the boudoir, emptied out some mixture, and replaced most of it by the poison. Then she locked the bureau, took the key back to Catherine, kissed her and said good-bye, hoping that when she came back from London, with her own death sentence pronounced, Aunt Catherine would no longer be alive to hear the news. After a few excited words with Hannibal, whom she met in the garden, though she gave him no hint of what she had done, she went back to her own house, where her daughter Muriel was waiting, and thence to the station and London.

We have only the specialist's account of what he said to Anne during the consultation. He was full of hope and reassurance, but could not make a definite statement without a further examination, and asked her to visit him again the following Monday. Little comforted, Anne returned to Macebury, expecting to hear on her arrival that the poison had had its effects. But no word came, and in the end she telephoned herself to Otho House. This was the call which Hannibal answered as we were going to bed. He described it to me as Maria Hall's, lest I should be surprised at his talking to Anne so late at night. He had already a suspicion of the violence of her feelings towards him, and was anxious, for her sake as well as his, that no one should learn of it.

On Saturday morning, Aunt Catherine took the fatal dose, and it was I who gave the news to Anne. It was not till the deed was done that she considered the chance of others being implicated. In the afternoon she came round to Otho House ostensibly to see me. While I was having my second interview with the police, she had a talk with Hannibal, and learnt not only that he was under suspicion, but also that he had tampered with the desk during the night, in his search for the stolen letters. This was an act which she had not allowed for, and her distress was so great that she nearly lost all self-control.

Sunday passed miserably. On Monday she had her second visit to pay to the specialist, who told her—and again we have only his version—that while he saw no reason to share in her alarm, he could not feel quite satisfied about her till she had spent a month in his clinic, both for treatment and observation. This continued suspense was in itself sufficient to make Anne hysterical, but hardly had she left the doctor's when she saw a poster announcing my uncle's arrest. I am not clear as to her later movements in London. She did, however, catch the train due at Macebury at 7.44. On arriving, she went to the waiting-room, and sat there for nearly three-quarters of an hour. I have often tried to imagine her feelings during these minutes, and think of her as one in a nightmare, bewildered with a thousand memories, while alternate moods of ecstasy and despair swept through her with such violence that when, at last, she did what she had resolved she must do, the act, in comparison with her thoughts, seemed petty and of little consequence.

At half-past eight, a thick scarf round her neck, her little hat pushed well over her eyes, she went to the police station and asked to see Glaize. When he came to her, she told him that she wished to make a statement regarding the death of Mrs. Cartwright, and asked him to take down what she was about to say. Glaize called a constable into the room as witness, and himself wrote down what she dictated. Her confession was full and concise. By way, not of extenuation, but of explanation, she referred to her own ill-health which had made her desperate, and her conviction that many people, especially her own daughter, would be better off for Catherine's death. Glaize was shrewd enough to ask how exactly Catherine's death would help Augusta. To this Anne replied that Augusta, although not a favourite of her aunt's, would probably find enough settled upon her to enable her to live in comfort, and that even if she did not benefit under the will at all, sufficient money would come to the Carvel family to maintain her. Had Glaize pressed the point further, he might have realised that this motive by itself was insufficient. Perhaps he intended to ask other questions later. When, finally, Anne had finished her confession, and had heard it read aloud to her, she rose and signed it, and while Glaize was about to arrest her, with an embarrassed formality, she pulled out a pistol which she had been grasping in her left hand beneath her scarf, put the muzzle in her mouth, and fired. She died at once. At the autopsy, no trace of disease was found in the body.

Appendix B

The Case against Hannibal Cartwright

ON looking back, I cannot say when I first began to suspect Anne of being the criminal. I should like to think that as soon as I had cleared Uncle Hannibal to my own satisfaction, my intuition at once fastened upon her. Unfortunately, it turned to Dace, and, when difficulty of motive seemed to rule him out, it hovered about vaguely. Even when I realised from reading my mother's letter that Aunt Fanny might have sent a bottle to Macebury and thus broken down the alibi based on the purchase at Bales', Anne only occurred to me as a name on a list which I must revise. Indeed, it was not till I had found Aunt Catherine's letter and read the section in the medical book devoted to oxalic acid that the real possibility of Anne's guilt came home to me. I then regarded Uncle Hannibal as an accessory—probably an unwilling one —after the fact, and conceived of his situation as still full of peril. When Glaize came to the Carvels' house, I knew he had bad news, but I naturally did not know whether the police had traced the crime to Anne by their own skill or whether she had confessed. I slipped away, during the painful confusion which followed my uncle's return to the dining-room, as quickly as I could. Indeed, I ran almost the whole way to the Golden Crane, and locked myself in my bedroom.

I did not burst into tears as I had after Aunt Catherine's death, though I was far more moved by what must have happened. I sat in a stupor for half-an-hour, trembling and with damp hands, then hid my evidence as well as I could, and went downstairs to the deserted lounge. There I found a telegram from my mother, saying, "How absurd you are. Of course I have not taken any of the stuff and will not."

This made me calmer, though, of course, I had already ceased to regard Aunt Fanny as a poisoner, and I sat, again reading the agricultural paper, till a quarter past ten. I then went to the station to see if my confidential adviser was coming. I forgot that I had no means of identifying him, and even when I saw one man, and one man only, walking with a small suitcase towards the hotel, I followed foolishly behind, not daring to accost him. Indeed, it was he who first spoke to me in the lounge, identifying me, I suppose, by my furtive and expectant glances. He was about thirty-five, sandy-haired, and thick-set. I liked him, and, as soon as we had privacy, lost no time in telling him the whole story. He listened patiently to my digressions and at some points made my narrative more precise by asking questions.

At the end he said, "Do you wish me to watch Mr. Cartwright's interests?"

"Yes," I answered, "as far as they still need it."

"From what you have told me, I am sure they still need it."

He was right, and I learnt afterwards that in spite of Aunt Anne's confession and suicide, the police were disposed to suspect Uncle Hannibal of complicity. The Carvels were so appalled at the disaster that they had no heart to press the charge further. I do not think Terence ever completely understood how far his wife had fallen in love with Uncle Hannibal, and if Glaize suspected it he did not show signs of knowledge. Uncle Hannibal's finger-prints on the bureau, the wrapper, and the bottle had, of course, to be explained away by the story of Jessie Toler and Alf's threatening letters. As to this, Colles obtained valuable corroborative evidence. Jessie was with child, but the father was Dace's brother, who was a footman in the house where she was employed. The blackmailing scheme was largely devised by Dace. The letters had been written by his brother in Alf's name. The real Alf Toler had gone to Canada six months before. The relations between my aunt and Dace seem to have been very intimate, and, though I do not suggest any kind of impropriety, I think it may well be that she found him attractive and was very ready to listen to him when he brought her tales of her husband.

Dace was also responsible for the disappearance of the wrapper. He had picked it up in the first place, in the course of his duties, and later, when he realised the value set on it by the police, concealed it, in the hopes that it would one day be a source of revenue. Uncle Terence, with great acuteness, thought it possible that Dace had it, and obtained it from him by brow-beating and cajolery on Sunday night, when he was one of the visitors whom I saw from the drawing-room window.

Uncle Hannibal had actually left a print on the stopper of the bottle. It was very faint and blurred by Aunt Catherine's prints and was not noticed till a special expert had examined it. It was the expert's discovery of this which led to my uncle's arrest on Monday morning.

As to the objects which I found in the tree, my uncle's account, given privately to Colles and me, is that on the Friday night, when he was searching in the drawing-room desk for Alf's letters, he noticed in an unlocked drawer a bottle of the mixture, in unbroken wrappings, bearing Bales' stamp. He also saw, in the blotting paper in the same desk, my aunt's unfinished letter to Aunt Fanny, which he read in case it shed any light on his own troubles. Naturally, neither discovery meant anything at all to him at the time. But later he was in a position to know, first, that my aunt had bought a bottle at Bales', and secondly, that this bottle could not be the one to contain the poison; for it was still unopened in its cardboard box. I have often thought how different the whole case would have been if Dr. Bradford, before showing any sign of suspicion, had asked him where and when Catherine had got the bottle. He would almost certainly have answered that he thought Fanny had sent it, and that there was a duplicate bottle downstairs. As soon as the facts of my aunt's death were brought home to him, he realised that the letter to Fanny and the unopened bottle might be of vital importance; for he expected the police to assume, as they did, that the poisoned bottle in the bureau was the bottle bought at Bales'. Indeed, he was determined that no one should think otherwise, and had even deceived me, during his confession on the Sunday night, by giving me to understand that he knew Catherine had bought the bottle at Bales' through the messages which she had given him for Anne—while, in reality, there had been no such message, and his knowledge of the different origins of the two bottles arose from his discoveries.

His early suspicion of Anne and his chivalrous wish to protect her are equally clear, and I now regret asking him, as I did more than once, whom he first suspected of being the murderer. At first he would only say, "You," but later he admitted that, though "suspect" was too strong a word, he had felt uneasy about Anne.

"You must have known," I said, "that the longer the poisoned bottle was known to have been in the house, the more people would have had the opportunity to put the poison in. In other words, suspicion would have been less concentrated on you—and on me—if you had shown the police Fanny's letter. Why didn't you?"

"I don't know."

"Then, the medical book. When did you read it?"

"When you were upstairs with the doctor."

"Why did you hide it?"

"Because I didn't want you to read it."

"In case I should suspect Anne?"

"Yes."

"Then you suspected her?"

"I thought you might."

It was unkind and needless to probe too far. As to Anne's motive, he knew of Augusta's trouble, and he knew also, I am convinced, that Anne would do almost anything for him. He was not in love with her.

What would he have done, I asked once, if he had been brought to trial and sentenced to death?

"I suppose," he said, "I should have produced the letter and the bottle then. My nerve would have given way."

Perhaps he knew that Anne would not have let him die.

The police very nearly charged him with being an accessory after the fact, but they had not evidence enough to do so. On Colles' advice, we put *Forensic Medicine* back on its shelf and said nothing about it. The bottle and the letter to

Aunt Fanny we had to produce, in order to corroborate Anne's confession. The first question the police asked was, "Where is the bottle bought at Bales'?" and it had to be answered. My uncle maintained resolutely to the police that he had hidden the bottle in the tree in order to protect himself. When asked how he thought he was protecting himself, he could only plead that he had reasoned foolishly, and had obeyed a blind instinct to conceal all the facts he could, just as he had concealed his innocent raid on the bureau. Whatever Glaize may have thought, he declared himself satisfied. The police in London had shortly before made a mistaken arrest, and the papers were very full of it. It may have been partly owing to this that the authorities, having a victim in the body of Anne Carvel, were willing to let matters rest. We, for our part, were not eager to bring any action in respect of Hannibal's wrongful detention.

Appendix C

AFTER THE CASE

THE inquest on Tuesday was formal. I gave my evidence— a less terrifying ordeal than I had feared—and the doctors gave theirs. A verdict was returned to the effect that Aunt Catherine had died through oxalic acid poisoning, though there was not evidence enough at that stage to show how it came to be administered. Aunt Catherine was buried on Wednesday morning. Uncle Terence did not come to the funeral. Bob and I were the chief mourners. Bob was accompanied by his sister Hetty, "swinging her hips like any harlot," as I overheard Maria Hall say. She was there with all the Dennises, purposeful and elaborately respectable.

In the afternoon of the same day there was the inquest on Anne Carvel. It was very painful. Terence had to go into the box and give evidence about his son-in-law's affairs.

"Was the deceased right," he was asked, "in thinking that you intended to turn your daughter adrift, if Sir James Teirson could not extricate himself from his—er—difficulties?"

"Oh, no. Good God, no."

The answer produced a good impression.

"But you had shown yourself unsympathetic to your daughter's troubles?"

"I'm afraid I must have done. I had no sympathy with my daughter's husband. If she had left him, of course—if she had been thrown on her own resources . . ."

At this point he broke down, and the pale green eyes were filled with tears like little glass beads.

Hannibal left England as soon as he could for Biarritz, where he bought and managed a large garage. I am to visit him there next summer.

Bob and I administered Aunt Catherine's estate, with the help of Smoult and the Dennises. I need not go into the details of our task. Otho House was put up to auction and bought by three ladies, who intended to turn it into a girls' school. I attended the sale with a concealed joy.

Finally, the proceeds were doled out, or grouped in packets of trustee securities, the income of which was monotonously paid to the appropriate beneficiaries. My mother was delighted with the extra money, but was soon spending up to the hilt. She made me an allowance, and I moved to a larger flat, which cost so much more than my old rooms that I felt little better off. Aunt Fanny became queen of Bude. Of my thousand pound legacy, I spent some and invested the rest in British Celanese at four and a quarter. At the time of writing this, the shares are barely two.

THE PERENNIAL LIBRARY MYSTERY SERIES

Delano Ames

CORPSE DIPLOMATIQUE   P 637, $2.84
"Sprightly and intelligent."

           —*New York Herald Tribune Book Review*

FOR OLD CRIME'S SAKE   P 629, $2.84

MURDER, MAESTRO, PLEASE   P 630, $2.84
"If there is a more engaging couple in modern fiction than Jane and
Dagobert Brown, we have not met them."   —*Scotsman*

SHE SHALL HAVE MURDER   P 638, $2.84
"Combines the merit of both the English and American schools in the
new mystery. It's as breezy as the best of the American ones, and has
the sophistication and wit of any top-notch Britisher."

           —*New York Herald Tribune Book Review*

E. C. Bentley

TRENT'S LAST CASE   P 440, $2.50
"One of the three best detective stories ever written."

           —Agatha Christie

TRENT'S OWN CASE   P 516, $2.25
"I won't waste time saying that the plot is sound and the detection
satisfying. Trent has not altered a scrap and reappears with all his old
humor and charm."   —Dorothy L. Sayers

Gavin Black

A DRAGON FOR CHRISTMAS   P 473, $1.95
"Potent excitement!"   —*New York Herald Tribune*

THE EYES AROUND ME   P 485, $1.95
"I stayed up until all hours last night reading *The Eyes Around Me,*
which is something I do not do very often, but I was so intrigued by the
ingeniousness of Mr. Black's plotting and the witty way in which he spins
his mystery. I can only say that I enjoyed the book enormously."

           —F. van Wyck Mason

YOU WANT TO DIE, JOHNNY?   P 472, $1.95
"Gavin Black doesn't just develop a pressure plot in suspense, he adds
uninfected wit, character, charm, and sharp knowledge of the Far East
to make rereading as keen as the first race-through."   —*Book Week*

Nicholas Blake

THE CORPSE IN THE SNOWMAN   P 427, $1.95
"If there is a distinction between the novel and the detective story (which
we do not admit), then this book deserves a high place in both categories."   —*The New York Times*

THE DREADFUL HOLLOW   P 493, $1.95
"Pace unhurried, characters excellent, reasoning solid."
                                        —*San Francisco Chronicle*

END OF CHAPTER   P 397, $1.95
". . . admirably solid . . . an adroit formal detective puzzle backed up
by firm characterization and a knowing picture of London publishing."
                                             —*The New York Times*

HEAD OF A TRAVELER   P 398, $2.25
"Another grade A detective story of the right old jigsaw persuasion."
                                —*New York Herald Tribune Book Review*

MINUTE FOR MURDER   P 419, $1.95
"An outstanding mystery novel. Mr. Blake's writing is a delight in
itself."   —*The New York Times*

THE MORNING AFTER DEATH   P 520, $1.95
"One of Blake's best."   —Rex Warner

A PENKNIFE IN MY HEART   P 521, $2.25
"Style brilliant . . . and suspenseful."   —*San Francisco Chronicle*

THE PRIVATE WOUND   P 531, $2.25
[Blake's] best novel in a dozen years . . . . An intensely penetrating study
of sexual passion. . . . A powerful story of murder and its aftermath."
                               —Anthony Boucher, *The New York Times*

A QUESTION OF PROOF   P 494, $1.95
"The characters in this story are unusually well drawn, and the suspense
is well sustained."   —*The New York Times*

THE SAD VARIETY   P 495, $2.25
"It is a stunner. I read it instead of eating, instead of sleeping."
                                        —Dorothy Salisbury Davis

THERE'S TROUBLE BREWING   P 569, $3.37
"Nigel Strangeways is a puzzling mixture of simplicity and penetration,
but all the more real for that."   —*The Times Literary Supplement*

Nicholas Blake *(cont'd)*

THOU SHELL OF DEATH   P 428, $1.95

"It has all the virtues of culture, intelligence and sensibility that the most exacting connoisseur could ask of detective fiction."

—*The Times* [London] *Literary Supplement*

THE WIDOW'S CRUISE   P 399, $2.25

"A stirring suspense. . . . The thrilling tale leaves nothing to be desired."

—*Springfield Republican*

THE WORM OF DEATH   P 400, $2.25

"It [The Worm of Death] is one of Blake's very best—and his best is better than almost anyone's."   —Louis Untermeyer

John & Emery Bonett

A BANNER FOR PEGASUS   P 554, $2.40

"A gem! Beautifully plotted and set. . . . Not only is the murder adroit and deserved, and the detection competent, but the love story is charming."   —Jacques Barzun and Wendell Hertig Taylor

DEAD LION   P 563, $2.40

"A clever plot, authentic background and interesting characters highly recommended this one."   —*New Republic*

Christianna Brand

GREEN FOR DANGER   P 551, $2.50

"You have to reach for the greatest of Great Names (Christie, Carr, Queen . . .) to find Brand's rivals in the devious subtleties of the trade."

—Anthony Boucher

TOUR DE FORCE   P 572, $2.40

"Complete with traps for the over-ingenious, a double-reverse surprise ending and a key clue planted so fairly and obviously that you completely overlook it. If that's your idea of perfect entertainment, then seize at once upon *Tour de Force.*"   —Anthony Boucher, *The New York Times*

James Byrom

OR BE HE DEAD   P 585, $2.84

"A very original tale . . . Well written and steadily entertaining."

—Jacques Barzun & Wendell Hertig Taylor, *A Catalogue of Crime*

Henry Calvin

IT'S DIFFERENT ABROAD   P 640, $2.84
"What is remarkable and delightful, Mr. Calvin imparts a flavor of satire
to what he renovates and compels us to take straight."

—Jacques Barzun

Marjorie Carleton

VANISHED   P 559, $2.40
"Exceptional . . . a minor triumph."
—Jacques Barzun and Wendell Hertig Taylor, *A Catalogue of Crime*

George Harmon Coxe

MURDER WITH PICTURES   P 527, $2.25
"[Coxe] has hit the bull's-eye with his first shot."

—*The New York Times*

Edmund Crispin

BURIED FOR PLEASURE   P 506, $2.50
"Absolute and unalloyed delight."

—Anthony Boucher, *The New York Times*

Lionel Davidson

THE MENORAH MEN   P 592, $2.84
"Of his fellow thriller writers, only John Le Carré shows the same
instinct for the viscera."   —*Chicago Tribune*

NIGHT OF WENCESLAS   P 595, $2.84
"A most ingenious thriller, so enriched with style, wit, and a sense of
serious comedy that it all but transcends its kind."

—*The New Yorker*

THE ROSE OF TIBET   P 593, $2.84
"I hadn't realized how much I missed the genuine Adventure story
. . . until I read *The Rose of Tibet*."   —Graham Greene

D. M. Devine

MY BROTHER'S KILLER   P 558, $2.40
"A most enjoyable crime story which I enjoyed reading down to the last
moment."   —Agatha Christie

Kenneth Fearing

THE BIG CLOCK   P 500, $1.95

"It will be some time before chill-hungry clients meet again so rare a compound of irony, satire, and icy-fingered narrative. *The Big Clock* is . . . a psychothriller you won't put down."   —*Weekly Book Review*

Andrew Garve

THE ASHES OF LODA   P 430, $1.50

"Garve . . . embellishes a fine fast adventure story with a more credible picture of the U.S.S.R. than is offered in most thrillers."
                                —*The New York Times Book Review*

THE CUCKOO LINE AFFAIR   P 451, $1.95

". . . an agreeable and ingenious piece of work."   —*The New Yorker*

A HERO FOR LEANDA   P 429, $1.50

"One can trust Mr. Garve to put a fresh twist to any situation, and the ending is really a lovely surprise."   —*The Manchester Guardian*

MURDER THROUGH THE LOOKING GLASS   P 449, $1.95

". . . refreshingly out-of-the-way and enjoyable . . . highly recommended to all comers."
                                —*Saturday Review*

NO TEARS FOR HILDA   P 441, $1.95

"It starts fine and finishes finer. I got behind on breathing watching Max get not only his man but his woman, too."
                                —Rex Stout

THE RIDDLE OF SAMSON   P 450, $1.95

"The story is an excellent one, the people are quite likable, and the writing is superior."   —*Springfield Republican*

Michael Gilbert

BLOOD AND JUDGMENT   P 446, $1.95

"Gilbert readers need scarcely be told that the characters all come alive at first sight, and that his surpassing talent for narration enhances any plot. . . . Don't miss."   —*San Francisco Chronicle*

THE BODY OF A GIRL   P 459, $1.95

"Does what a good mystery should do: open up into all kinds of ramifications, with untold menace behind the action. At the end, there is a bang-up climax, and it is a pleasure to see how skilfully Gilbert wraps everything up."
                                —*The New York Times Book Review*

Michael Gilbert (cont'd)

THE DANGER WITHIN   P 448, $1.95
"Michael Gilbert has nicely combined some elements of the straight detective story with plenty of action, suspense, and adventure, to produce a superior thriller."   *—Saturday Review*

FEAR TO TREAD   P 458, $1.95
"Merits serious consideration as a work of art."
         —The New York Times

Joe Gores

HAMMETT   P 631, $2.84
"Joe Gores at his very best. Terse, powerful writing—with the master, Dashiell Hammett, as the protagonist in a novel I think he would have been proud to call his own."   —Robert Ludlum

C. W. Grafton

BEYOND A REASONABLE DOUBT   P 519, $1.95
"A very ingenious tale of murder . . . a brilliant and gripping narrative."
         —Jacques Barzun and Wendell Hertig Taylor

THE RAT BEGAN TO GNAW THE ROPE   P 639, $2.84
"Fast, humorous story with flashes of brilliance."
         —The New Yorker

Edward Grierson

THE SECOND MAN   P 528, $2.25
"One of the best trial-testimony books to have come along in quite a while."   *—The New Yorker*

Bruce Hamilton

TOO MUCH OF WATER   P 635, $2.84
"A superb sea mystery. . . . The prose is excellent."
     —Jacques Barzun and Wendell Hertig Taylor, *A Catalogue of Crime*

Cyril Hare

DEATH IS NO SPORTSMAN   P 555, $2.40
"You will be thrilled because it succeeds in placing an ingenious story in a new and refreshing setting. . . . The identity of the murderer is really a surprise."   *—Daily Mirror*

Cyril Hare (cont'd)

DEATH WALKS THE WOODS P 556, $2.40
"Here is a fine formal detective story, with a technically brilliant solution demanding the attention of all connoisseurs of construction."
—Anthony Boucher, *The New York Times Book Review*

AN ENGLISH MURDER P 455, $2.50
"By a long shot, the best crime story I have read for a long time. Everything is traditional, but originality does not suffer. The setting is perfect. Full marks to Mr. Hare." —*Irish Press*

SUICIDE EXCEPTED P 636, $2.84
"Adroit in its manipulation . . . and distinguished by a plot-twister which I'll wager Christie wishes she'd thought of."
—*The New York Times*

TENANT FOR DEATH P 570, $2.84
"The way in which an air of probability is combined both with clear, terse narrative and with a good deal of subtle suburban atmosphere, proves the extreme skill of the writer." —*The Spectator*

TRAGEDY AT LAW P 522, $2.25
"An extremely urbane and well-written detective story."
—*The New York Times*

UNTIMELY DEATH P 514, $2.25
"The English detective story at its quiet best, meticulously underplayed, rich in perceivings of the droll human animal and ready at the last with a neat surprise which has been there all the while had we but wits to see it." —*New York Herald Tribune Book Review*

THE WIND BLOWS DEATH P 589, $2.84
"A plot compounded of musical knowledge, a Dickens allusion, and a subtle point in law is related with delightfully unobtrusive wit, warmth, and style." —*The New York Times*

WITH A BARE BODKIN P 523, $2.25
"One of the best detective stories published for a long time."
—*The Spectator*

Robert Harling

THE ENORMOUS SHADOW P 545, $2.50
"In some ways the best spy story of the modern period. . . . The writing is terse and vivid . . . the ending full of action . . . altogether first-rate."
—Jacques Barzun and Wendell Hertig Taylor, *A Catalogue of Crime*

Matthew Head

THE CABINDA AFFAIR   P 541, $2.25
"An absorbing whodunit and a distinguished novel of atmosphere."
—Anthony Boucher, *The New York Times*

THE CONGO VENUS   P 597, $2.84
"Terrific. The dialogue is just plain wonderful."
—*The Boston Globe*

MURDER AT THE FLEA CLUB   P 542, $2.50
"The true delight is in Head's style, its limpid ease combined with humor
and an awesome precision of phrase."   —*San Francisco Chronicle*

M. V. Heberden

ENGAGED TO MURDER   P 533, $2.25
"Smooth plotting."   —*The New York Times*

James Hilton

WAS IT MURDER?   P 501, $1.95
"The story is well planned and well written."
—*The New York Times*

P. M. Hubbard

HIGH TIDE   P 571, $2.40
"A smooth elaboration of mounting horror and danger."
—*Library Journal*

Elspeth Huxley

THE AFRICAN POISON MURDERS   P 540, $2.25
"Obscure venom, manical mutilations, deadly bush fire, thrilling climax
compose major opus.... Top-flight."
—*Saturday Review of Literature*

MURDER ON SAFARI   P 587, $2.84
"Right now we'd call Mrs. Huxley a dangerous rival to Agatha Christie."   —*Books*

Francis Iles

BEFORE THE FACT P 517, $2.50

"Not many 'serious' novelists have produced character studies to compare with Iles's internally terrifying portrait of the murderer in *Before the Fact,* his masterpiece and a work truly deserving the appellation of unique and beyond price." —Howard Haycraft

MALICE AFORETHOUGHT P 532, $1.95

"It is a long time since I have read anything so good as *Malice Aforethought,* with its cynical humour, acute criminology, plausible detail and rapid movement. It makes you hug yourself with pleasure."

—H. C. Harwood, *Saturday Review*

Michael Innes

THE CASE OF THE JOURNEYING BOY P 632, $3.12

"I could see no faults in it. There is no one to compare with him."
—*Illustrated London News*

DEATH BY WATER P 574, $2.40

"The amount of ironic social criticism and deft characterization of scenes and people would serve another author for six books."
—Jacques Barzun and Wendell Hertig Taylor

HARE SITTING UP P 590, $2.84

"There is hardly anyone (in mysteries or mainstream) more exquisitely literate, allusive and Jamesian—and hardly anyone with a firmer sense of melodramatic plot or a more vigorous gift of storytelling."
—Anthony Boucher, *The New York Times*

THE LONG FAREWELL P 575, $2.40

"A model of the deft, classic detective story, told in the most wittily diverting prose." —*The New York Times*

THE MAN FROM THE SEA P 591, $2.84

"The pace is brisk, the adventures exciting and excitingly told, and above all he keeps to the very end the interesting ambiguity of the man from the sea." —*New Statesman*

THE SECRET VANGUARD P 584, $2.84

"Innes . . . has mastered the art of swift, exciting and well-organized narrative." —*The New York Times*

THE WEIGHT OF THE EVIDENCE P 633, $2.84

"First-class puzzle, deftly solved. University background interesting and amusing." —*Saturday Review of Literature*

Mary Kelly

THE SPOILT KILL P 565, $2.40
"Mary Kelly is a new Dorothy Sayers. . . . [An] exciting new novel."
—*Evening News*

Lange Lewis

THE BIRTHDAY MURDER P 518, $1.95
"Almost perfect in its playlike purity and delightful prose."
—Jacques Barzun and Wendell Hertig Taylor

Allan MacKinnon

HOUSE OF DARKNESS P 582, $2.84
"His best . . . a perfect compendium."
—Jacques Barzun & Wendell Hertig Taylor, *A Catalogue of Crime*

Arthur Maling

LUCKY DEVIL P 482, $1.95
"The plot unravels at a fast clip, the writing is breezy and Maling's approach is as fresh as today's stockmarket quotes."
—*Louisville Courier Journal*

RIPOFF P 483, $1.95
"A swiftly paced story of today's big business is larded with intrigue as a Ralph Nader-type investigates an insurance scandal and is soon on the run from a hired gun and his brother. . . . Engrossing and credible."
—*Booklist*

SCHROEDER'S GAME P 484, $1.95
"As the title indicates, this Schroeder is up to something, and the unravelling of his game is a diverting and sufficiently blood-soaked entertainment."
—*The New Yorker*

Austin Ripley

MINUTE MYSTERIES P 387, $2.50
More than one hundred of the world's shortest detective stories. Only one possible solution to each case!

Thomas Sterling

THE EVIL OF THE DAY P 529, $2.50
"Prose as witty and subtle as it is sharp and clear. . .characters unconventionally conceived and richly bodied forth . . . . In short, a novel to be treasured."
—Anthony Boucher, *The New York Times*

Julian Symons

THE BELTING INHERITANCE   P 468, $1.95
"A superb whodunit in the best tradition of the detective story."
                                        —August Derleth, *Madison Capital Times*

BLAND BEGINNING   P 469, $1.95
"Mr. Symons displays a deft storytelling skill, a quiet and literate wit,
a nice feeling for character, and detectival ingenuity of a high order."
                                        —Anthony Boucher, *The New York Times*

BOGUE'S FORTUNE   P 481, $1.95
"There's a touch of the old sardonic humour, and more than a touch of
style."   —*The Spectator*

THE BROKEN PENNY   P 480, $1.95
"The most exciting, astonishing and believable spy story to appear in
years.   —Anthony Boucher, *The New York Times Book Review*

THE COLOR OF MURDER   P 461, $1.95
"A singularly unostentatious and memorably brilliant detective story."
                                        —*New York Herald Tribune Book Review*

Dorothy Stockbridge Tillet
(John Stephen Strange)

THE MAN WHO KILLED FORTESCUE   P 536, $2.25
"Better than average."   —*Saturday Review of Literature*

Simon Troy

THE ROAD TO RHUINE   P 583, $2.84
"Unusual and agreeably told."   —*San Francisco Chronicle*

SWIFT TO ITS CLOSE   P 546, $2.40
"A nicely literate British mystery . . . the atmosphere and the plot are
exceptionally well wrought, the dialogue excellent."   —*Best Sellers*

Henry Wade

THE DUKE OF YORK'S STEPS   P 588, $2.84
"A classic of the golden age."
  —Jacques Barzun & Wendell Hertig Taylor, *A Catalogue of Crime*

A DYING FALL   P 543, $2.50
"One of those expert British suspense jobs . . . it crackles with undercur-
rents of blackmail, violent passion and murder. Topnotch in its class."
                                        —*Time*

Henry Wade (cont'd)

THE HANGING CAPTAIN P 548, $2.50

"This is a detective story for connoisseurs, for those who value clear thinking and good writing above mere ingenuity and easy thrills."

—*Times Literary Supplement*

Hillary Waugh

LAST SEEN WEARING . . . P 552, $2.40

"A brilliant tour de force." —Julian Symons

THE MISSING MAN P 553, $2.40

"The quiet detailed police work of Chief Fred C. Fellows, Stockford, Conn., is at its best in *The Missing Man* . . . one of the Chief's toughest cases and one of the best handled."

—Anthony Boucher, *The New York Times Book Review*

Henry Kitchell Webster

WHO IS THE NEXT? P 539, $2.25

"A double murder, private-plane piloting, a neat impersonation, and a delicate courtship are adroitly combined by a writer who knows how to use the language." —Jacques Barzun and Wendell Hertig Taylor

Anna Mary Wells

MURDERER'S CHOICE P 534, $2.50

"Good writing, ample action, and excellent character work."

—*Saturday Review of Literature*

A TALENT FOR MURDER P 535, $2.25

"The discovery of the villain is a decided shock." —*Books*

Edward Young

THE FIFTH PASSENGER P 544, $2.25

"Clever and adroit . . . excellent thriller . . ." —*Library Journal*

If you enjoyed this book you'll want to know about
THE PERENNIAL LIBRARY MYSTERY SERIES

Buy them at your local bookstore or use this coupon for ordering:

Qty	P number	Price
	postage and handling charge	$1.00
	_____ book(s) @ $0.25	
	TOTAL	

Prices contained in this coupon are Harper & Row invoice prices only.
They are subject to change without notice, and in no way reflect the prices at
which these books may be sold by other suppliers.

**HARPER & ROW, Mail Order Dept. #PMS, 10 East 53rd St., New
York, N.Y. 10022.**
Please send me the books I have checked above. I am enclosing $_____
which includes a postage and handling charge of $1.00 for the first book and
25¢ for each additional book. Send check or money order. No cash or
C.O.D.s please

Name_____

Address_____

City_____ State_____ Zip_____

Please allow 4 weeks for delivery. USA only. This offer expires 12/31/84.
Please add applicable sales tax.